HAZED

GRETA T. BATES

This is a work of fiction. Names, characters, places, and incidents are products of the author's imagination or are used fictitiously and are not to be construed as real. Any resemblance to actual events, locations, organizations, or persons, living or dead, is entirely coincidental.

World Castle Publishing, LLC
Pensacola, Florida
Copyright © 2025 Greta T. Bates
Hardback ISBN: 9798285019091
Paperback ISBN: 9798891264106
eBook ISBN: 9798891264113
First Edition World Castle Publishing, LLC, June 24, 2025
http://www.worldcastlepublishing.com

Licensing Notes

Cover: Adam Martin
Editor: Karen Fuller

"One taste of the poisoned apple and the victim's eyes will close forever in the Sleeping Death."

-Snow White 1937

CHAPTER 1

NOW

It was the end of September. Well past Labor Day. The days were long, and the sunsets stunning. Trudy and I were officially seniors. I can't say it was an easy transition, but considering my summer, starting the school year had gone as well as it could. I am 18 now. My injury all healed up. My course load was easy. I only needed to go to class for half a day to fulfill my graduation requirements. T and I were attending full moon gatherings at *Mystic Blue* with Kelly and the Girls. Hell, I had my own freaking house! Some things were good. And some things…not so much. I was still in therapy. And the pills. Yeah, they were prescribed, and yeah, I needed to sleep and to function daily. Still, I was taking pills. I hated to admit it. The whole thought of taking something in the morning and something at night altered my state of mind. It just…it kept me tied to my lineage. I couldn't help but think that I, too, was one of The Horrifying Women. And, oh, that one still living member of The Horrifying Women—Mom was still on lockdown. I hadn't made any trips back to The Spa.

T and I saw each other every day. We had most of our classes together. At lunch, we'd take off either to T's to eat and work on assignments, hang out making art, or talk about our lack of love lives, or some days, we'd head downtown and poke around *Blue*, talking Kelly's ear off, asking about, "What crystal is good for this?" or "What incense is good for that?" Other days, we'd sit in the coffee shop for hours, sipping our lavender lattes and playing the underwear game. The underwear game—pretty simple, really—we'd just watch the door and whoever entered, guy or gal, we'd take turns guessing what color or kind of underwear they were wearing. Just a lame way to pass the time. Amusing but lame.

I'd gotten a job at said coffee shop. Next door to *Blue* was *BB's*. Not part of a chain but a sister location to the island's *Beach Bum's Bakery*. A mother/daughter team ran *Beach Bum's*, and I think the mom had an aunt or a cousin or something, someone who wanted a bit of the island feel in our quaint, coastal town. I applied for a job right before the semester had started. My stepdad was paying my way right now, but I still wanted to help out how I could and have some money of my own. Right now, T and I were still "kids on bikes" like the groups of teens in the thriller/horror genre that would pedal their way to saving the day, but I wanted some wheels. Shit, I *was* 18. It was about damn time.

I had zero experience making fancy ass coffee. I had to train for a couple of weeks, but I had the hang of things now. I could work all the equipment and I could even make some pretty cool designs with the steamed milk. Plus, *BB's* set my schedule around school and my therapy sessions. These days, there was no stigma to being in therapy — it's almost expected, necessary selfcare. And when I was off, T and I took advantage of my employee discount.

Today was just an ordinary day. T and I had done the usual — left school for the day, popped into *Blue* for some cinnamon incense supposed to improve concentration and focus, and then grabbed coffee to go from *BB's*. Then, it was over to T's to work on an art project that was due later next week.

In T's kitchen, my head stuck in the fridge, I hollered, "Hey, bestie. What should I pick to munch on?" T had filled her parents in on what had gone down after my birthday, my stepdad moving out, Mother's insane act of self-cannibalism, and my venture back into therapy. They'd sort of unofficially adopted me after that—su fridge was mi fridge.

"Oh...just get the carrots and celery my mom cut up and the black bean hummus."

That was T, trying to keep me healthy, mentally and physically. Back at my place, I favored chips and diet drinks, but here, I'd give into exploring more food groups and try to blend in. Like I'd said in the past, at T's house, I didn't want to fuck things up.

"Right," I said, "I see them." I grabbed the veggies in one hand, the hummus in the other, and shut the door with my hip. She was standing there, hands extended to grasp anything I needed help carrying.

T was ready for fall. Today, she was dressed

head to toe in shades of autumn: from the top of her chin-length copper do—she'd kept the bob—to her pumpkin latte-colored jumper, down to her chestnut tights and dark brown loafers. She looked like some sort of version of the Sapphic queen, Velma from Scooby Doo, just cooler, well...a little bit cooler.

Once in T's room, I kicked off my Docs, lost my long black wrap-around skirt, and sat crisscross apple sauce in my holey leggings and my "Don't Dream It, Be It" Rocky Horror t-shirt—come late October, we were sooo going to the midnight show this year! We spread out on the floor, side by side, with our snacks and all of our stuff. We were each working on a project. The first in a long line leading up to a final senior art piece. The projects were supposed to be self-portraits with a twist. T just couldn't decide which decade she'd like to represent, and from what I could see over her shoulder, she was playing around with the 20s, herself in a Great Gatsby-esque fringed number. I, on the other hand, had gone in another direction. I'd been trying to draw an apple, a distorted carved face, mine, similar to a jack-o-lantern, the eyes, the mouth, openings revealing not a worm on the inside, but all kinds of multicolored capsules spilling out from the orifices.

"Nice imagery, Elia," T said, now looking over my shoulder, "Nothing like art imitating life, I say." That was T's nice way of trying to compliment what I was doing and not say what I think she was probably thinking, *Oh brother, Elia. Yeah, yeah, the pills are like poison. Fairy-tale much?*

I started to erase what I was doing. Maybe I needed to put a little more thought into this. After all, school projects could raise red flags if I got too real. I was already in therapy. I didn't want to be whisked away to a remote location with padded walls. "It's just an idea, a work in progress," I said, ready to change the subject, "Anyway, with it being the first day of fall and all, maybe we should spend some time thinking about, oh, I don't know…the Harvest Dance? I mean, shit, I know we never go to stuff like that, but it *is* our senior year. Maybe we should consider…"

I barely got the words out of my mouth when T squealed and pulled a mood board out from under her bed, plopping it down on the floor in front of us. "Elia," T said, "I've been waiting, hoping you'd bring this up!"

After an hour of listening to T go on about velvet and tulle, contemporary designs or 60s glamor a la *Valley of the Dolls*, dates or no dates, I decided I'd had enough. I loved T and all, but fashion was not my jam. Hugging T bye, I headed out into the late afternoon swelter that was September in the south.

The days were still long. It was a glorious afternoon. Today. You could never tell this time of year. We were right in the middle of hurricane season. There were even storm days built into our school calendar in case we lost power and internet or roads were impassable. It's happened before, and it could happen again. That was one thing I did not like about living alone—storms. Trudy's family was my family, though, and I knew I could always go over there in the event of severe weather warnings. But not tonight. Tonight, I'd revel in my aloneness and enjoy the solitude.

As I got closer to home, I braced myself. I remembered that nothing had happened in a long time, though. I hadn't felt the grip of my ancestor's hands — The Horrifying Women — reaching out for me since the summer. I made it to the front door, greeted by bags of groceries. Every once in a while, my stepdad would have food delivered. He'd even throw in a bottle of wine. It wasn't for me. I didn't care much for alcohol. We had an understanding. I used it every night in my evening ritual.

It was good of him, my stepdad, still looking out for me. Maybe he believed me about the visits, and maybe he didn't, but if he didn't, he supported my delusions, nonetheless. I'd make the bottle of red last until the next delivery, carefully measuring out a little each night. Like I said, it wasn't for me. It was for Aunt Laera.

I brought all of the bags into the kitchen, plopping them on the counter and setting out the wine and a small glass. I fumbled around in the junk drawer near the fridge, pulled out a corkscrew, and set it down near the glass. I thought about dinner, but the thought left my mind as quickly as it had come. I'd eaten some over at T's, and these days, with the stress of senior year, the heat, and, of course, the meds, I didn't have much of an appetite. Now, it was time for a long, hot bath, studying, and the ritual. Then, it was pop my pills and head off to a dreamless sleep.

As I lay in the tub, steam filling the room, I thought back to Aunt Larea's first appearance in this very room. She had made contact and scared the shit out of me. But after everything went down last summer, there'd been no hair pulling, electrical surges, shapes darting around corners—nothing except for that last time in the attic. And I'd put an end to that quickly enough. Kelly had put me in touch with a couple of local sisters who specialized in hauntings. I had the ladies over with Kelly, of course. They brought in equipment, ghostometers, and the like, explored the house from top to bottom, and detected energies here and there. The Spector Specialists sat me down, offered their assistance, and summed up the situation. They pretty much said the only one of the spirits still hanging around was Aunt Laera. She had unfinished business. Well fuck. They asked me if I knew anything or had any information, and I just shook my head no. Then, they performed a blessing of the property and a protection spell (yeah, they were ghostologists, but they were also women of the woo). And before

they left, they taught me a ritual. It had helped. I
just didn't know how long the peace would last
until Aunt Laera made another appearance, letting
me know just what "business" she still had to take
care of.

 After my bath, I got into bed, surrounded
by my purple walls, music on low, and studied for
a test I had coming up at the end of the week. My
eyes drifted over to my desk and the bottles of pills
lined up in a row, the pharmaceutical version of
a witchy spice rack. Something like lavender, to
relax. Something like valerian for sleep. Something
uplifting like peppermint in case I was in too much
of a fog for school or work, but I never took that
one. I'd never needed to rev up. Only they weren't
herbal remedies, which I hated. I didn't want to
be like her, like Mother. I hoped therapy would be
temporary and I could transition from my meds to
a more natural means of navigating my ups and
downs. At least if I needed long-term therapy, shit,
I knew it was probably inevitable. You're never
cured of addiction. You just have to learn to use
better tools to manage your life. And I was willing
to learn. I would never, ever be like Mother, with

her self-medication, be it sedation or sweets.

THEN

I don't remember exactly when I realized Mother was on medication. I'd just accepted it. If I had to pick a year, or a time, I would say it was when I was in early elementary school. As a little kid, I noticed her behavior was changing. She had her good moments in the beginning, some I could hold onto — they were few and far between; it was back when I still called her Mama. But as time went by, those 'good days' gave way to mood swings and the rearing of her horrible temper, and she became Mom, then Mother.

Then, there was the change. Or I should say changes. Yes, as I got older, I noticed that Mother consistently took pills for this or that. Pills replaced the binging. The days, the sad days when Mom would scarf down an entire cheesecake. The days of the pills — she was never into putting in any kind of effort or work to 'get better,' be it physically or mentally. But the Xanax, this was the one, the one that altered her the most. On the day of, she'd be that Stepford Wife. She would clean, prepare meals, and even read to me sometimes. Mom would have her shit together on those days. She was downright cheerful; dare I say happy. I almost didn't recognize her on those days. After all, she'd be smiling. I wasn't used to that.

But...but...then there would be the days when she became someone else. These were the days when she was off her meds, Xanax specifically. The day after she took it, if she didn't take another one, those would be the bear days. After a while, we, my stepdad and I, knew when this other Mother would show up. Our first clue would be her dress, her hair—she did NOT have her shit together on these days. My stepdad began to disappear on those days. Me, I was a kid, sure, later after I'd become friends with T, I could make myself scarce, escape. Before that, though, I got really good at ducking—flying furniture, drinking glasses, and the back of her hand. I learned to move fast.

NOW

Enough studying for one night. I went down and checked the front door, and turned on the porch light. Then, I headed to the kitchen to get ready. I pulled the shears out of the junk drawer and snipped a sprig of rosemary from the pot near the window above the sink. Next, I poured a glass of water for myself and a small glass of red wine. I flipped a few switches, turning out unnecessary lights. I took the glasses and the rosemary with me up the stairs. I set everything down on my desk. First, I took my nighty night pills, swallowed them down. The bathroom was next.

Washing my face, and brushing my teeth then, it was time for the ritual. Since this was the first room I'd ever seen Aunt Laera in, it was the logical place to make the offering, though none of this was *really* logical. The Specialists had given me clear instructions. A small piece of rosemary for protection and the wine. Spirits liked spirits. Every night since I'd met these other women of the woo, I performed this act. And it was working. You see, there are rules in any practice, and the ghosts apparently followed the rules, too. Maybe they had a guidebook like in *Beetlejuice*, 'a handbook for the recently deceased?' Anyway, in the mornings, the wine was gone, and I'd put the leftover rosemary out back in the yard in the compost. Aunt Laera may have had unfinished business here, but she was behaving at present. And now, I'd hurry to get into the bed. I'd started to feel the now familiar feeling of my meds doing their thing. The fog was rolling in.

CHAPTER 2

I woke up feeling rested. I always did now with the help of my meds. It was Friday and I needed to get to school and then over to *BB*'s—I had the afternoon shift today. Not a bad gig working at the coffee shop. Besides my discount on my days off, I got free coffee and food during my shift which was super cool, never having to think about dinner on those nights. My chop job from the summer was growing out, and my blue-black layers had gotten longer, forming a bob that was just below my chin. I put on my sunset-colored work t-shirt, letting it hang over one of my long black flowy skirts and the puka shell necklace T had given me. It was a beachy look. And a headband, not that I liked that, but I had to keep my hair out of my face for work. T would definitely notice my attempts at accessorizing—such a rare event. Stopping in the kitchen, I reached for a Diet Coke and a handful of granola. Then, stepping into my Docs, I was out the door.

T and I had said our see ya's after our last

class. Tomorrow was Saturday, though, and I'd see her, Kelly, and the Girls for a full moon gathering after closing time at *Blue*. It was close to the autumn equinox, and the September moon was called the Corn Moon. It had only been a month or two since T and I had started meeting with the Woo Woo Girls, and we were still learning about the different moon phases, the names, and other stuff like that. T didn't turn 18 until next April, but the Girls either didn't know or didn't care.

Before I entered *BB's*, I had to pass by some of the sulky teenagers that lined this street in front of *Blue* and the coffee shop — how they could stand hanging out on the sidewalk, all in black in this heat, I didn't know. I just figured they must want those clove cigarettes pretty fucking bad. The group gathered today were the girls T and I called The Satanic Six. We'd seen them at school. They were transplants, kids from out of state, who'd started at our high school during our sophomore and junior years — all from different places, yet they had gravitated towards each other last year, becoming one single, dark unit. Their leader, we secretly called Doc because we thought she was a dealer, was sitting on the ground right next to the door in an herbal-scented cloud of smoke, legs outstretched. I'd have to say something or try to step over her to get in. I chose to clear my throat.

"Ahem," I managed. Doc lifted her head at this, her black-lined eyes, the color unclear, locking with my light blue ones. She pursed her equally dark lips and slowly folded her legs in with an eye roll. The others didn't look up or budge, heads down, scrolling away, chipped noir nails click-clacking on their screens. In a low-key exasperation, I went in for my shift, knowing I'd have to wait on one or all of them later, wishing they would just go away. I could wish.

The coffee shop was buzzing. It was Friday afternoon, and some extended their lunch hours to include late "meetings" at *BB's*. You know, pretend to be all about work but really starting their weekends early. As I hung up my bag in the back, an older lady all in black with bleach-streaked shoulder-length hair, her arms full of binders, passed by me, mumbled an "Excuse me," and was out the front door.

"Who was that?" I asked Tristan. Tristan was

one of my co-workers, about 30 or 35, divorced, using this barista gig as additional income.

"Oh, that was Miss Bentley, Bennie. She's the owner. Bennie is Barbara senior's cousin, you know, over on the island, owner of the original BB's?"

"Wow. Never met her."

"Yeah, Bennie has a small place here but she doesn't get to this side of the bay much. Just came in today to work on some paperwork, accounts to go over. Stuff like that."

I just nodded in silence. I knew that would be the extent of our work conversation today. Tristan looked tired. Her work t-shirt was rumpled, her jeans with stains here and there, and pieces of hair escaping her dated scrunchie. Shit, I would be tired too—single mom, three kids, working two jobs. The dick head ex-husband left her high and dry. Tristan was pretty much all business, just clock in, work, clock out. No chumminess. No work relationships. No messiness.

I'd been running the steam wand, so I didn't hear them come in. Doc and three of her side kicks. The other two must have slithered home. Doc and

Bitchy ordered espressos and Mouse, the shy one, a cold brew with almond milk. The one who seemed the least grumpy, T and I called Oh Joy, asked for a lavender latte.

"Hey," I said, "That's what I usually get too. They're yummy." Yummy? I'd said, "Yummy?" For a minute, I'd forgotten these girls acted as one, that Oh Joy was probably just like the rest of them.

Doc and the gang took their drinks and split without paying. I was pissed! But Oh Joy hung back, reached into her black studded bag, and pulled out a card. I ran it and said, "Thanks," as she slipped a few bucks into the tip jar. Taking her drink, she inhaled the heady aroma of the brew, then took a sip, the froth leaving a trace mustache on her upper lip.

"Mmm...I love the smell of lavender," she said as she looked at me, lapping away the foam. Her eyes, what were they, hazel? Some shade of green? Amber? I couldn't quite place the exact color.

I watched her walk away, her long, pink-tipped onyx waves swinging, grazing the waist of her black jeans. Then, Oh Joy turned around.

"I always end up paying...rich parents," she said, shrugging. I smiled a little at this.

"I'm Elia," I offered.

"Hi, I'm Aurora, but everybody calls me Ro...See you later...maybe?"

Was that a question or a statement? I wondered. Lifting my hand to wave, I opened my mouth to say something, but she'd already left, the door closing behind her.

After dark, I headed home from work to an empty house. T had plans with her parents, so it would just be me tonight. The usual. I went to the kitchen, poured a glass of wine, and made myself a cup of tea. Going up the stairs to my room, I thought, "*Oh shit.*" I'd forgotten the rosemary. I turned, went back, cut a small twig, and then went up to my room, stopping in the hall bath to put the wine and the rosemary out for Aunt Laera.

It wasn't too late. I decided to savor my tea and stream some old horror movies. The lights out, a blanket pulled over my knees, I sipped my tea. I'd decided on *The Craft* — 90s teen witchy stuff. I'd taken my meds right before I hit PLAY, hoping to stay awake for most of it. About a third of the way in, my eyes became heavy. I set my cup on the side table before I nodded off completely.

The next morning, my laptop was still open. I stretched and let out a big yawn. Had I finished the movie? Or was that a dream? Somehow, I think my sleeping mind had mixed up the girls from *The Craft* with The Satanic Six. Had I dreamed about all of them? Or had it just been Oh Joy, I mean, Ro. She had a name now. She seemed nicer than the rest of them. Of course, I'd never spoken to the others, so maybe they were all different? It probably wasn't nice of me and T to come up with nicknames for all of them: Doc, Bitchy, Oh Joy, er Ro, Mouse, Couch, and Cola. Shit, they may have worse names for me and T! Teenage girls — they more than likely did.

It was the full September moon and tonight was a gathering. I had really started looking forward to these events. I was already close with T, and it felt like Kelly and the Girls had adopted me. They were my new family and a far cry from The Horrifying Women I was actually related to. I looked up to the Girls and I wanted to be prepared tonight. I had a nice collection of woo woo books now, and I thought I'd go through them today and read about the moon, the equinox, and stuff like that. The Corn Moon represented the harvest, so spells for abundance, gratitude—they fit the bill. Summer moving into fall, so anything to do with change would be appropriate, too. THAT was probably what I needed—CHANGE. After the summer I'd had, what went down with Mom at The Spa, yeah, change would be nice.

Around 5 o'clock, T and I met at the crossroads of Bay Breeze Way and Myrtle Lane to walk over to *Blue* together. The sky was yellow, and the wind was picking up, tree limbs swaying, leaves shivering. There was a storm brewing in the Gulf. Even though I felt ok about living at home alone, T's parents had made me promise that in the event of severe weather, I'd go to their house. That was the plan.

There was T—feather earrings, a long flowy dress, and a cream-colored shawl—she was all Stevie tonight. I was in a dress from my black Goodwill collection with a beat-up cross-body messenger bag that held my woo woo books. "Hey," T said as she greeted me with one of her best hugs. "What? Is this it tonight?" she asked as she tugged at my dress and then gave me a smile and her best twirl. The "white witch" homage was not lost on me.

"Nope," I said, "See?" And with that I tucked my ebony bob behind my left ear to reveal a hint of glitz, some vintage sparkly earrings I'd picked up on my last thrifting score.

"Nice! Color me impressed. Should we knock…"

But before we could, Kelly had magically appeared at the door.

Kelly was dressed in one of her maxi jersey numbers, red tonight. Hair now black as jet piled atop her head, a huge hunk of moldavite hung between her breasts. And she had new plugs in her gauges with some kind of triangle configuration on them. Hey! They matched the tattoo she had on the inside of her left arm. I'd totally forgotten about asking her about that! It must mean something.

Kelly took us in the back. T and I slipped out of our shoes while Kelly smudged us. I could hear the ladies talking and carrying on. The room was set up as usual with an altar and, tonight, a circle of chairs around it. All the Girls were there: Mary,

Shirley, Bee Bee, and Miss Constance donning their sunset-shade resort wear. And there were two others, the sisters, both dressed in head-to-toe deep eggplant, flowy pants, and tank sets.

"You remember Iris and Joyce, right, Elia?" Kelly offered.

Iris and Joyce? Iris and Joyce? I had such a hard time remembering names. Shit. I'd only recently stopped identifying the Girls by their boxed hues.

"Yes, of course," I said, "Iris and Joyce."

Fuck. Were The Ghostly Gals twins, and I'd never noticed or bothered to learn their names? The shit I went through over the summer had really done a number on me. The time Kelly brought them over to my house seemed like a dream. Ok. One had slightly shorter hair than the other. Now, I'd just have to figure out which was which. Just then, another lady came in, bumping into me. It was the lady in black from the coffee shop, her flaxen hair just meeting her shoulders. I turned and came face to face with my boss I'd never met, Miss Bentley.

"Oh, I'm so sorry, hon. It seems I'm always

in such a rush. I'm Bentley, but everyone calls me Bennie," she said to no one in particular. Then, she looked back at me.

Her face—smile lines creasing her forehead and the edges of her emerald eyes, skin tan from too much sun, the corners of her mouth upturned like a cat with a secret—was kind, and I couldn't place her age.

"Hi," I said, "I'm Elia. Actually, I work for you at *BB's*."

"Oh, oh, oh. Yes, of course, Elia! I'm sorry we haven't met before. Like I said, I'm always in high gear, flying here and there."

I just smiled uncomfortably. My eyes worked the room, me, T, Kelly, the Girls, The Spook Team, and now Bennie. Our circle was growing. At this, my smile became more genuine.

"It's time," Miss Constance said. Mary took her place near the altar in the center of the room. Bee Bee, Miss Constance, Shirley, and Kelly took their places in the four corners. Me, T, and the new girls stood in front of the chairs within the circle. Mary lit her sage bundle and began to walk the circle, calling directions. She began near Kelly welcoming in the energies in the east, representing the element of air. Before she could move on, an alert began to sound, first on one phone, then intermittently on all of our phones. T and I looked at each other and then down at our phones. A second later, we all looked at Mary.

"Well, girls," Mary started, "Looks like the storm is indeed headed our way. Notification says maybe a Cat 3 or 4 when hitting land. It's time to prepare quickly."

The once tropical depression had turned into a full-blown hurricane. That was the end of the gathering tonight as we moved fast, righting the room, helping Kelly secure the shop—living in the south, we all knew what to do, and we didn't waste any time. Standing on the sidewalk outside *Blue*, we said our goodbyes at 1326 Bay Breeze Way as Kelly locked up. In a blur of colors, all the gals dispersed. T and I began to walk towards my house.

"I just need to pack a bag real quick and get my meds, you know," I was telling T, "and close the shutters." Thank Goddess for the hurricane shutters my stepdad had installed after a rough storm had gone through last season.

"Ok," T answered, "Just make it fast!" I could tell her voice was shaking. T was not a fan of big storms. Still, she pitched in and helped me batten down the hatches.

I texted my stepdad and told him what I'd done and where I'd be. We still connected every once in a while, and it was nice to have someone from my family on my side, even a little. Once I had my stuff and felt like things at the house were as good as they were going to get, T and I began to walk to her house. As I reached the sidewalk, I looked back at my house. I didn't feel the pull of the ghostly fingers of my ancestors. For a moment, I thought I saw one of the shutters open and then quickly close. I figured my anxiety was running high tonight. No time for my nightly ritual, I mentally crossed my fingers and let out a deep breath, hoping the house would remain undisturbed by the storm and from anything or *anyone* else.

T and I had passed the crossroads and were close to her house. We were rushing a bit as the weather was getting worse when I lost my footing.

I caught myself before I fell, but a few of my things flew out of my bag and onto the ground. I waved T on, bent down to get my stuff and it was then I saw her. It was only for a second. She had darted behind a tree when I'd turned around. What was she doing out here in this weather? Had she followed us? No, it wasn't one of The Horrifying Women coming back to taunt me. It was one of The Satanic Six. I'm sure it was the ringleader, Doc. I saw a lit cigarette tossed out from nowhere. The glow catching my eye, the butt eventually landing in a puddle, the smell of cloves lingering in the air.

CHAPTER 3

T and I settled in at her house and rode the storm out. Her parents had been great—we'd had a hurricane watch already this season, but it was nothing like this! The storm—Hurricane Francis—decreased in strength and had dropped from the anticipated Cat 3 or 4 to a 2, but our little coastal town still had a lot of damage. We'd lost power and phone service temporarily but like I said, Trudy's parents were prepared. They had a gas run generator for the house installed two years ago after the last bad storm, and everything was back up and running in no time. Everything we needed anyway: lights, AC, the fridge, the stove. We had it made compared to a lot of people.

Our school hadn't suffered any physical damage, nothing structural, no water in the buildings. Of course, they were waiting on power and Wi-Fi, and the buses couldn't run because of fallen trees and shit in the more rural areas, so school was closed, but the Superintendent had hopes of getting back up and going in a few days or so. We were reduced to local radio for any info. They'd get the power up quickly, I was sure, and the day after the storm, trucks were already running, removing limbs and debris, and clearing roads. Hell, the Cajun Navy had even arrived! I didn't know if that was because our mayor had good plans in place or if our little town wouldn't stand for ugly, maybe both, but more likely the latter.

Two days had passed. We felt full as ticks from filling ourselves with all of the many pantry items T's mom had stocked for bad weather. Boredom hit a peak. T and I decided to take a walk downtown to survey the damage. The coffee shop was unscathed. Then, we looked at *Blue*. The shop hadn't been so lucky. The front door was blocked off. From the outside, it looked like the roof had caved in. We peered in the windows. The lights were off, and we could see daylight streaming in from what used to be the intact ceiling. Seemed like definite water damage but no sign of any people. My heart broke for Kelly and what it would take to fix all of this.

I walked over and looked in the windows at

BB's. The lights were on, and there were a couple of people inside behind the counter. My hands pressed against the glass, thinking out loud, I said in an audible whisper, "Oh fuck, T. I haven't even thought about work during all of this. I better go in and see what's up."

"At least the sign on the door says *Closed,*" T offered. "Maybe they are just getting things ready, you know, to reopen?"

I looked at my friend, shrugged, took a deep breath, and headed inside. Nothing looked amiss—floors and tables were clean, but there was no music playing, and I didn't smell any coffee brewing. Then, Tristan popped her head up from behind the counter.

"Hey, Elia. Wow! That was some storm, huh? I just came by to see if I could help Bennie get ready to open up again. Of course…I have no help myself." I just nodded.

It was then I heard the sounds of kiddos. Tristan's kids must be playing around in the back.

"Ah," I said, my eyes darting side to side not meeting hers, understanding the situation but not offering to babysit or anything. Nope. Not taking the bait. I felt sorry for Tristan, but little kids were not my jam.

"Since we didn't have any damage, I won't be here long, so no worries," Tristan said, her mouth a tight line. "Bennie said we'd open back up tomorrow. People need us. For coffee and, well, for escape. For some sense of normalcy. She's in the back if you want to check in with her."

"Thanks," I nodded and went in the back, stepping over the gaggle of children, one coloring, the others glued to screens playing video games.

I saw Bennie dressed all in black, most of her hair in a lopsided top knot, her back to me, leaning over her desk. Wait. What was that on her neck? Did she have a small tattoo? What the…? It was the same symbol Kelly had—a triangle with a single circle inside. I needed to find out what the heck it meant.

"Oh…Elia," she said before turning around, "How are you, hon? I am *so* sorry," she said like she was choking up. She faced me, drawing me into an uncomfortable hug.

I had no idea what was going on. I pulled back from her. "I'm fine, Bennie. I stayed with

Trudy and her parents. We had everything we needed, so I'm okay, okay?"

"Oh, but Elia. The shop. *Blue.*"

"Oh, that," I said, "I saw the roof and water damage. I'm sure Kelly will have to close for a while. Maybe we can start a "Go Fund Me" for her and pitch in to set things up right again."

Bennie just looked at the floor, then up at me, her green eyes welling with tears. "Oh…you don't know."

"Don't know what?" What the fuck was going on?

"It's Kelly. She went back to the shop after we all left the other night. She was in the shop trying to set up sandbags when the storm hit. Then, the roof… oh, Elia. Kelly was injured badly. She's in a coma. Things don't look good. I am so, so sorry, hon."

My breath caught in my throat. Old wounds began to throb. The room began to tilt. Kelly… Kelly…Kelly. My head was spinning, my knees weakening. I was heading down. Then, everything went dark.

When I came to, Bennie and T were hovering

over me. Tristan had gathered up her crew like a mother hen and told T what had happened on her way out. T was holding my hand and sniffling. Bennie, eyes closed, was rocking forward and back and muttering something I couldn't make out.

"Elia!" T exclaimed, "Thank goodness!" And then, she scooped me up, hugging me tight. All at once, Bennie stopped what she was doing, the trance broken.

"Oh…Elia! Yes, thank goodness you are back with us! Now, let's see if you can make it over to one of the tables."

I looked at T, then back at Bennie. I smelled coffee now. What had happened? Did I pass out? Puzzled, I let them lead me to the front room, T sitting down with me while Bennie poured us all some coffee. Then…I remembered. I let out a howl like an injured animal, like a dog that had just been hit by a car.

"Kelly! My Kelly! Oh no! Oh no!" T pushed her chair closer to mine, holding me, weeping along with me. Bennie stood back and let us have our moment.

When T and I pulled it together, Bennie

brought over cream and sugar, and for a few minutes, we sipped our coffee in silence. After a bit, Bennie broke the quiet.

"Again, Elia, I am so, so sorry. I had no idea you didn't know. But now that I think about it, how could you? What with the storm and power outages."

I put my head in my hands and then looked up, my eyes red, tears still coming, spilling down my cheeks. "What are we going to do? How can we help her? Can I see her?" My thoughts whirling, I felt like I was babbling at this point.

"I don't know the answers to those questions, Elia. But I'll tell you everything I do know."

Apparently, Mary had called Bennie the morning after the storm. She was Kelly's emergency contact and had been called by the hospital after Kelly had been admitted. I guess some people still had phone service. The other gals, Bee Bee, Shirley, Miss Constance, and the ghost hunters—Iris and Joyce—all of them had left, evacuated for a while to stay with family out of state. Mary had tried to get in to see Kelly, but the hospital had strict regulations. The rule: only immediate family.

"What!" I was outraged. "We *are* her family!"
I said, slamming my fist against the table. Then,
under my breath, I added, "She is *my* family."

"Now, Elia. Mary, you, none of us are blood
relations to Kelly. Unfortunately, that's the way it
is," Bennie said.

"Well, I've got to try. I've just got to! She
needs to know she's not alone."

"Elia, I don't know if she'd even know you
were there, hon. I told you...it doesn't look good.
Why don't you take a day or two, stay over with
T's family, then come back to work. It will do you
good, help get your mind off of things."

T patted my hand, finally speaking, "Bennie's
right. Let's go back to my house, Elia. Ok?"

I pulled my hand away from T's and gave
her a what-the-fuck look. T gave me a pitiful look—
you would have thought I'd slapped her. Kelly's
family. T's family. Take a day or two. Sure. That's
all it would take. Get back to normal?? Things were
definitely *not* normal. I exhaled. Shit. I couldn't do
this to T, my brain battling my emotions.

"Alright," I said, trying to compose myself,
"I'll go." T brightened at this. "But, just to get my

things. I'm going home to *my* house." My emotions won.

T started to object, but I held up my hand, "Nope, no changing my mind, T. I need to be alone."

I caught a look pass between her and Bennie. Bennie didn't know all of my story but any sane person would know I didn't *need* to be alone right now. But in *my* mind, I was doing the right thing. Bennie hugged T, then me. I stiffened under her embrace. Leaving *BB's,* we opened the door to the sidewalk. Out of the corner of my eye, I could have sworn I saw someone rush around the corner, out of sight.

I smelled cloves again.

CHAPTER 4

Shit. Shit. Shit. I knew I had been rude to Bennie and a total bitch to T...but...Kelly. I couldn't get over the news of her accident. I'd apologize to Bennie when I went back to work, and I'd make it up to T. She always forgave me when I fucked up. But I knew, one of these days, I may use up all my chances with her.

No debris in the yard, which was weird. There was a fresh delivery of groceries near the front door. There was a note inside one of the bags. "Hey, Elia. Did you *weather* the storm ok? LOL. (Dad humor.) Please give me a call or shoot me a text...just let me know if you are ok." Groceries, *and* he'd picked up the yard, too. Care and concern from my stepdad. It was nice. The least he could do. And he always did the least. Fuck. I was sooo being a bitch today. Sighing, I picked up the bags and went inside.

Nothing seemed out of place, but I needed to look around anyway. Unloading the bags, I put the food and the wine on the counter, and then, opening the junk drawer, I snagged the ring of extra keys. I hadn't been up to my mom's room or the attic space since the summer. But…what the hell? I needed to get my mind off Kelly.

Standing before Mom's door, I sighed again as I turned the knob and went inside. Empty. Still. Nothing. Cold, though, unusual for September in the south. I crossed the floor and fumbled around for a few minutes, trying to remember which of these keys opened the small door. Ah. There we go. A few steps up, and I was in. It was colder in here. Doesn't heat rise? Nothing out of order. Everything was as I'd left it, the vanity, the box marked BOOKS, and the old trunk. I walked over to the box of BOOKS and then felt something tug my hair. "Ouch!" I couldn't help thinking, *"Is Aunt Laera making an appearance?"* I looked around, nothing. I smoothed my hair and knelt to open the box. "Ouch. Fuck." Again, with the hair pulling, ghostly fingers grasping errant black strands. Aunt Laera making her presence known. It wasn't as scary as the first time she'd done it, but it seemed… familiar.

THEN

Maybe I was two or three? Back when I still called her Mama. I don't know how I could remember that far back, but with Mother, I had pictures, few and far between, but pictures of the past, in my mind.

We were in a room I didn't recognize, moonlight streaming in through the window. And there was music. Or was it humming? Yes, Mother was humming. I was in her lap. She was rocking me to sleep. She would hum for a minute, gently stroke my hair, and then mumble to herself, her body tensing. Then, YANK. She'd pull my hair! It was a dance. Softly singing, brushing my fine baby hair, still golden in those days, then the muttering and YANK! SNATCH! Actually pulling my hair out! I'd cry out, and that just seemed to make her more stressed, spur her on, but I couldn't help it. I was just a little thing. In those early years, Mother would put hats on me when we went out in public.

NOW

My eyes brimming with tears, I remembered that The Twin Telepaths had told me that Aunt

Laera was sticking around for a reason. Wiping my eyes, I thought maybe *not* the box of BOOKS? Maybe I'm supposed to look in the trunk. "Is that it, Aunt Laera? The trunk?" Bending down, I placed my hand on the top of the trunk. Nothing. Still cold, but no action from the beyond. "Ok," I said protectively, putting my hair behind my ear. I opened the trunk, peering inside.

It was mostly junk, old, aged photos, a couple of pieces of vintage clothes, which I snatched up immediately, and a few smaller boxes. I grabbed one of the boxes, shoved the clothes under one arm, and shut the trunk. More to look at on another day when I felt adventurous. I went down the steps and into Mother's room, put the box on the floor, and closed the small door. Leaving my mom's attic room, I tried to just pull the door to with my foot, the door not quite closing, leaving a gap, and, WHOOSH, a blast of cold air raced past me into the hall. What had I let out?

Leaving the clothes and the box in my room, I went down to the kitchen. Time for the ritual, but...after today...I thought I'd join Aunt Laera for cocktail hour. Shit. I forgot I'd left the food out. I put away any perishable items and left the rest on the counter. Hell, it was just me living here anyway—easy access. I clipped off a rosemary stem and poured two glasses tonight. I deserved it after hearing about Kelly. I left the rosemary and one glass in the bathroom as usual. I didn't even bother with a bath or changing my clothes. I walked over to my desk and ran my fingers over my mini pharmacy, taking the "something like lavender" and the "something like valerian" and washed them down with a red blend. Brr. I shivered from "something like a cold draft."

As the pills were kicking in, I laid down, bringing the wine with me to bed. I sipped a little, cried a little. Rinse and repeat. I was thinking about Kelly, about how she'd been there for me, not once but lots of times. She was there for me before I knew I needed her, knowing I needed help the first time she'd seen me wander into *Blue*. She was there for me when I had questions about spells, herbs, and the like. She was there for me when I'd fucked up over the summer, intervening before I'd done any permanent damage to myself, urging me to go back to therapy. Even though she was more like a "cool aunt," Kelly had nurtured me, and been the mother I needed. And now… now…God, she just *had* to be ok. She *had* to pull through. I *had* to figure out a way to get to see her. Tears making tracks down my face, the wine glass slipped out of my hand. I was sooo sleepy. I was sooo dopey. I laughed a little (a little like a crazy person.) Yes, I was sooo dopey. As I drifted off, I felt something on the top of my head, like fingers running through my hair. A stroke. Only a soft, gentle touch, soothing me, comforting me. It wasn't long before I fell asleep, the scent of vanilla surrounding me like a security blanket.

~*~

Oof! I sat up too quickly. Ouch. My head hurt. I stayed on my bed for a minute, holding my face in my hands, trying to think back over the night. *"Is this what a hangover feels like?"* Ok. I know I'd taken my pills. Oh. And wine. I'd had my own glass of red as well as a pity party last night. Ugh. Only one glass, but obviously, I was a lightweight, and it probably didn't mix well with my meds. I felt like shit. Why do people do this on a regular basis? But I knew the answer. To *not* feel.

Piecing together the events of yesterday, I remembered performing my nightly ritual in the bathroom, oh, and going to the attic. I'd have to try on those vintage items I'd snagged from the trunk. The box.... I'd get to that later. And something else. I remember.... someone patting my head. But how? It *must* have been a dream. Sure, that had to be it. And Kelly. I remembered what had happened to Kelly. Getting up, I noticed the empty glass on the floor, evidence of the cause of my aching head. I needed to take something. Shit. I needed to focus. School wasn't opened back up yet since the storm, and I wanted to try to get in to see Kelly today.

I swiped some over-the-counter pain killers from my desk top pharmacy. Then, I picked up the bottle of "something like peppermint," the pills to pep you up. I'd never taken these, but I thought I needed them today. I went into the bathroom to pull myself together and flipped on the light switch. Geeze. Off again. Too bright. There was enough light coming in through the window to see what I needed to see. Jerking my head back, I attempted to swallow the pills. Turning on the faucet, I bent over, closed my eyes, and took two or three gulps of water from the tap. There now. I shut off the water and looked in the mirror. First, I saw the fright that was my reflection, and then I noticed that, as usual, the rosemary was on the shelf where I always left it, but the wine. The wine was still there! Oh shit, oh shit, oh shit. What *had* happened last night? I started to remember more, the attic, the cold draft, the fingers—not a dream?? I didn't think Aunt Laera was going to behave anymore. Maybe ghosts didn't always follow the rules. Fuck. Of course, they didn't! I'd stirred up something, some energy or something last night. And I knew she'd been hanging around for some reason, but what was it? I looked back in the mirror. She still wasn't showing herself. It was just me, hungover me. Then, I felt something on my tongue. With my fingers, I pulled out a long, gray strand of hair. I bent over again, ready to puke, and then I saw more, dangling from the faucet and pooling like a nest in the sink drain.

CHAPTER 5

I showered quickly and wrapped a towel around myself. I stayed as far away from the sink as I could, just dashing over to dump the wine into the hair nest. I'd deal with *that* mess later. The ritual. I'd try the ritual again tonight. But for now, I ran out of the bathroom, fighting the urge to hurl.

Still not feeling myself, I knew I had to get to the hospital today to try to see Kelly. I sucked in my lips, holding back my tears, threw on my usual head to toe black, and left the house. Coffee. I needed coffee. As I got to the edge of my yard, I felt the pull, the fingers. I hadn't felt them in a long time. Something was back, or *someone*. Maybe it was only Aunt Laera. Her I thought I could handle.

I got to the front door of *BB's*, averting my eyes from *Blue*—I just couldn't look over there. The sidewalk in front was clear of any signs of the storm and no sign of The Satanic Six either. I wondered if any of them had evacuated, gone back to the bowels of Hell?? I laughed to myself. I must be feeling a little better. There were a good many people in there, looking for Wi-Fi and coffee. Tristan was behind the counter and just lifted her chin in a 'sup greeting. Then, as if she could read my mind, moved her head to the side and back, somewhat glancing over her shoulder, indicating Bennie was in the back. I took a deep breath. I needed this job. Ready for my humble pie, I went to get a forkful, hoping I could stomach it.

Bennie had her head down and her hair down, working. Shit, I'd forgotten to research anything about that shape I'd see on her neck, the tat like Kelly's, the triangle circle thingy. She wasn't alone. Mary was back there with her. Before I could spend any time thinking about tattoos or anything, eyes not leaving the papers on the table, Bennie spoke.

"Hello, Elia."

That was it. Mary just sipped whatever she was drinking silently. Okay. The rest was up to me.

"Hi, Miss Bennie. What's up?" What's up? THAT was all I could muster?? Nothing but crickets. Okay, I'd try again. "Miss Bennie...I'm sorry...I'm sorry for the way I acted yesterday. It was childish. Okay, I know. I was a bitch. I took the information about Kelly personally. I'm sorry."

With that, I got a soft smile from Mary and then Bennie got up from the table. She faced me, smiled, and pulled me in for a hug, and I let her this time. "Oh, Elia. Thank you. I needed that. And no "Miss" Bennie. I know we're in the south, but please, no "Miss," k, hon?"

"Alright. I can do that or *not* do that." I looked over at Mary now. "You're back now, Mary. Any news on Kelly's condition? I want to go to the hospital today and see her."

"Well, I called the hospital late yesterday. There'd been no change, no improvement. And Elia, you can try but I don't think they're going to let you in to see her either. They are pretty strict about the 'immediate family' only rule."

"I've got to try. I need to see her with my own eyes."

"Well, hon, if you're set on it, go ahead, try. Just let me know when you'd like to come back to work. Your job is here when you're ready. Although Tristan may be ready for you to come back sooner rather than later." Bennie chuckled quietly under her breath.

"Oh, thank you, Mi—, I mean, thanks, Bennie! I'll be in tomorrow morning and if school is reopening, in the afternoon, k?"

She hugged me again, "No worries. And, hon? Make yourself a lavender latte on the way out," she said with a wink.

I gave Mary a quick hug bye and she whispered in my ear, "Good luck. May the Goddess be with you." With a single nod, I was gone.

~*~

The shop had gotten quiet. Tristan was leaning against the counter, looking down at her phone. I helped myself to a coffee, not wanting to take the time to make a special blend, and I noticed there were no go cups or lids. I bent down to get a cup from under the counter. I smelled them before I saw them—patchouli and clove. When I popped back up, there they were, The Satanic Six, all of them—Doc, Bitchy, Mouse, Couch, Cola, and Oh Joy, I mean Ro. Ro grinned at me from beneath her dark hair, behind side swept bangs with streaks of purple today matching her glossy lips. I got my coffee abruptly, spilling some in the process. I did *not* want to wait on them. Doc was drumming her fingers on the counter impatiently. I had to get out of there. Tristan looked up from her phone, I gave her a pleading stare, and with a huff, she slowly ambled over to take their orders.

I was almost out of the door when I heard a low, "Hey." I turned around, facing Ro, her amber eyes almost glowing.

"Hey," I said, "Sorry, I'm in a hurry today. I've got to get over to the hospital to see a friend."

"Kelly?"

"Ah, yeah. How did you…"

"I've been in *Blue* before. It *is* right next door, you know?"

"Oh…right. Of course."

Ro reached out, grabbing my hand. "I'm sorry," she said, and for just a moment before she pulled away, her pointy fingernails grazed my palm. With a slight grin, all I could do was nod, her amber eyes locking with my baby blues. Then, I took off. Yeah. All I could do was nod because when she touched me, my stomach did a flip, heat rose to my cheeks, and I couldn't speak…in a good way.

On the way to the hospital, my phone vibrated in my pocket. I had cell service again. Without looking, I knew it was a text from T.

Hey. C'est moi. What's up? Do you want to hang out later?

I started, then I stopped. I wasn't ready to see T yet. I felt like shit for how I'd acted the other day. I needed to let the dust settle. School would be opening in a day or two. Everything would be fine, just like always.

Ditching my coffee, I went into the hospital, head down, trying to appear inconspicuous, just in case Mary had been right, that only *family* could get in to see Kelly. Shit. I knew she was right, but I had to try. To me, Kelly *was* family and I had to lay eyes on her. I knew she had to still be in the ICU. It had only been a few days since the storm. I scanned the walls of the corridors for signs, walking in like I knew where I was going. Ah! ICU to the right.

First, I had to get past the nurses' station. They were busy gibber jabbering, one of them showing the others something on their phone. This was my chance. One door, then two, then the third — I was here at Kelly's room! I had to be quick. Still too close to getting caught and kicked out. I looked into the small, square window on the door, and there she was—bruised, bloodied, and bandaged. I gasped, then put my hand over my mouth to quiet myself. I'd gotten this far; I couldn't draw attention to myself. Kelly was hooked up to a lot of machines. With her eyes closed, her face looked calm and peaceful, but the rest of her...ok...she was mostly covered by a gown and a blanket, but I could see discolorations on her neck and chest under the multicolored wires keeping her...my God...conscious? Alive? I was biting down on my hand now to keep from crying out loud. Her arms were exposed. They were all marked up, with spots of dark red and purple, some blackened. She looked like she'd had the shit beaten out of her! I cast my gaze at my shoes for a second; I had to look away. When I looked back, I saw something else on the inside of her left arm, that tattoo, the one I'd seen on Bennie, the triangle with the circle inside. I *had* to remember to research that, find out what it meant. I glanced away again, this time at the nurses, seeing if I could slip inside the room. When I looked back at that small, glazed window,

I had a flash of the last time I'd been outside of a door just like this one.

THEN

My brain took me back, back to my last visit to The Spa and seeing Mother — the last of the *living* in the line of The Horrifying Women. I remember it all too well, my last look into that small, square window. It was a scene, man. Mother on the floor, flailing, screaming, her gown, her hands, stained, her face a hot mess, like a child who'd been eating ice cream with strawberry syrup at the park and needed their face wiped with a wet nap. Only it wasn't syrup; it was blood, her own, from the still hard to believe act she'd performed, cutting into her own leg, carving up a little snack, and chowing down. When she discovered I'd been cutting again, she couldn't be outdone. She had to have the spotlight. From the hall, I watched as the aides held her tight and knocked her out with liquid tranquility.

They'd moved Mother into a different ward after that. I don't know if my stepdad still visited, but I hadn't been back since that day. The Spa had called. Yes, my stepdad was the primary contact. I was the next in line. I know they'd been trying to contact us. One day, I didn't look at the caller id and answered by mistake. They'd had to amputate Mother's leg just below the knee as a result of an infection from her self-inflicted wound. Mother's nursey-nurse said they were trying to keep her calm and stop the problem from becoming worse, keep her from going septic. I thanked the woman, even though I was thinking, "*Yeah. Keep her calm. Good luck with that.*"

NOW

I was lost in my thoughts, and I didn't see or hear that nurse coming. I just felt a tapping on my shoulder, an insistent poking. Then, I came around and heard, "Hey, hey, excuse me, excuse me, miss? Are you here to visit the patient? Are you a relative, a *blood* relation?"

A blood relation? What the...? Being in the deep South, I'm surprised she didn't say kinfolk.

She reeked of cigarettes. The stench clung to her clothes. It was rank, sickening. I wasn't thinking too clearly today, and I couldn't come up with a lie fast enough. "No, ma'am. I'm not," I said, defeated. I muttered a "Sorry" to this nursey-nurse and left the hospital.

Wandering out into the sun, I let my feet lead me. It was such a strange time, what with so many places closed from the storm, and being on the outs with T. My T. I needed T. I had to find a way to make things right. When school opens back up, I know it will be easier. I'll see her between classes or at lunch and mumble some kind of apology. T would hug me and probably start getting carried away with the Harvest Dance and gushing about a dress or something. That is if the Harvest Dance was still happening.

I found myself heading home. The first thing I needed to do was to research that symbol, the tat I'd seen now on two women I knew. I'd use the modern witch's book of shadows—Google. As I neared the front walk, I felt that old familiar pull. The grip, the fingers drawing me in. I had thought The Horrifying Women were gone, most of them anyway. As I put my key into the lock, I felt other fingers, like someone stroking my head softly. This had happened before. Last night, in my wine/med confusion—I thought I'd imagined that! I jerked my head around, looking behind me. Nothing. Nothing but the smell of what, fresh baked cookies? I was losing it. God, Goddess, please don't let me end up at The Spa like Mom.

CHAPTER 6

The next day, I woke up groggy again. I did a repeat of the night before, wine and rosemary for Aunt Laera, wine and my "something for relaxation" and my "something for sleep" for myself. This morning, it would be my "something to uplift." I knew I was getting into a bad pattern, but life seemed uber tough right now, so I said, "Fuck it."

I looked at myself in the bathroom mirror. Man, I looked like crap on a cracker. Then, I noticed that Aunt Laera's wine was left untouched again. I poured the wine into the sink, the nest of hair gone thank God. I filled the empty glass from the tap and swallowed my meds. Now, downstairs to find something to munch on.

Sitting in a chair in the living room with my laptop and a cup of black coffee, I ate a banana, thinking that it was probably all I could get down. Slowly sipping, I took in the view. Yes, it was *my* house now, and yes, T and I had done some rearranging and really made my bedroom something special, but this room…this room still looked tired and had Mother's Southern touches here and there. The furniture was dated, and any antique pieces we had were now covered with a thick layer of dust. It was drab and dark. Although, I needed the dark this morning. Maybe I'd give this room a once over, and clean up. I could use a girl's night in with dinner and a spooky movie. A girl's night...T...my T. Ok. It was time. I needed to reconnect and put some feelers out to see if I was forgiven for my tantrum. And Ro. Maybe I could invite Ro over, too. That last time I saw her, I mean, shit, I hadn't felt an attraction to anyone for a long, long time. I'd like to feel that out, too.

I didn't know if the whole town had Wi-Fi yet since the storm. The phones had come back pretty quickly. Miracle of miracles, it was working! That most likely meant that school would reopen soon, and I'd have the perfect opportunity to eat some humble pie again and see T. Opening my emails, sure enough, there were several from the school, the latest one stating classes would resume tomorrow. I was going back to work this afternoon, but right now, I was ready to go down a rabbit hole, consult the Google Grimoire, and find out what the hell that circle with a triangle symbol meant.

It didn't take me long to find it. There were two versions of the symbol. One, ok, a circle within a triangle with a line through it was some Harry Potter bs. There was tons about that! But the circle within a triangle with no line — that one came from geometry and was something about an incircle or inscribed circle and blah, blah, blah, math language. Thanks, Wikipedia. If I knew Kelly, there had to be more to this than math.

I poured myself a second cup of coffee and kept looking. I'd typed in "circle within a triangle symbol." Then, I added "witch" and "occult." Bingo! Here. This was more like what I'd thought I'd find — The Order of Lilith. I didn't know anything about Lilith, so I went down another rabbit hole. Lilith has been called many names: vampire, demon, night owl, hag, the devil's wife, the first woman…the first …witch. Whoa. Shit. Now, I was getting somewhere! I went back and searched "The Order of Lilith."

{Once thought of as destroyer, monster, murderer of newborns, the legend of Lilith has been altered over time. Kicked out of the Garden of Eden for insubordination, her story began as told by men. The first wife of Adam, banished, a woman to be feared, a killer. Modern witches have reclaimed her and follow The Order of Lilith. No longer enemy of women but now known as nurturer, warrior, and Queen. Like Kali, Lilith is fierce. She balances the scales and seeks justice. Still destroyer but protector as well. Now, women tell her story, for women.}

    Wow! Just Wow! This was all so interesting. I read and read some more, then I realized I'd been scrolling for over an hour. Shit! I had to get ready to go to work. I put on the vintage dress I'd found in the attic over a pair of worn-out leggings. The dress was a light charcoal color with small pearl buttons down the front and had a drop waist. The hem was slightly frayed, just hitting my ankles. It had a Victorian vibe. Cool. It fit. It was roomy, but I liked that. I smashed a black felt hat over my unruly hair—a cut would be needed soon, or maybe I'd grow it out. I'd ask T about this. She knew more about this stuff, hair, clothes, etc. T. I felt a pang in my chest. I had to make things right with her. But now, I was late, so I pulled on my boots and walked over to *BB's*.

The shop was jumping. Things seemed back to normal, as normal as they could be after a hurricane. Tristan looked beat, her hair in a sloppy top knot bound by another dated velveteen scrunchie, two of her kids at a table on tablets, another under her feet behind the counter. She took one look at me in my new-to-me dress, a scowl forming, her face screwed up like she'd eaten a handful of Sour Patch Kids. "Oh," I thought, "She's pissed."

"Hey there," I said in a sing-song voice, trying to lighten the mood.

"Hey yourself, and thanks for coming in, finally. No work top today?"

Yep. She was pissed. "I'm sorry. I really didn't think we'd be busy again this soon. Just thought I'd wear something...different. Sorry."

"Oh. It's fine. I'm fine. Just handling it all, as usual."

I'm fine never meant "I'm fine." That was girl talk for F U bee-otch.

"I got it. Go. Take a break," I said, instantly

regretting that, wishing I could take hold of those words and pull them back into my mouth. If there was room with my foot in there.

"Oh. How *nice* of you for giving me permission to take a break. But really, I've got to do more than take a break. School starts back tomorrow. Daycare is reopening. I've got lots of shit to do. You got this, for real?"

I nodded, moving as fast as I could to get behind the counter and take over. Tristan herded her kiddos and was out the door in a huff. I didn't blame her for being mad. She had a tough life and no help. I made a mental note to try to make this up to her later somehow. Any way I could, except for babysitting.

Things were hectic for a while but then settled down. I took the lull to clean up and wipe tables. Heck, at one point, I even played the underwear game in my head to pass the time. Guy in the button-down and khakis: tighty whities. Blond, put together soccer mom: black lace thong for sure. Guy with guitar: plaid boxers. That one really wasn't fair. I could see the waistband creeping up out of his cargo pants. I started to wonder if other people played this game. If they were looking at me, thinking: Grungy Molly Ringwald, day of the week panties, wrong day, elastic shot.

The next thing I knew, I felt a hand on my shoulder. It was Bennie. Had she been here the whole time? I chatted with her for a few minutes, telling her about my visit to see or to try to see Kelly. She let me go on, never interrupting my flow. Then, she held up a hand to stop me.

"Elia, you've been through a lot the past few days, and I know you're all on your own at home. School starts back in the morning. You did a great job this afternoon. The shop looks good. Why don't you take off? I'll lock up."

"Uh, ok? Thanks, Bennie," I said as I let her hug me. I was trying to get used to it.

As I entered my empty house, I realized Bennie was right. I am all on my own. I put a frozen cheese pizza in the microwave, cut a piece of rosemary, and poured two glasses of wine. And then, I poured one of the glasses down the sink and opted for a diet soda. I could *not* self-medicate. I *would* not let myself. I had to fight it. I wouldn't become one of The Horrifying Women in my line. I know I had the genes for it. No princess life for me, no queen would emerge. No trying to be the star. I had to learn to let people in. I had to…soften, reign my bitchy-ness in. The first thing I was going to do was make up with T.

CHAPTER 7

School was starting back today. It seemed weird to start in the middle of the week. Hell, it always seemed weird after a hurricane, and now it felt like I was starting my senior year all over again, even though we'd been back since August. So, yeah, weirdness. And what with everything else going on, Kelly in the hospital, my dust up with T, and God knows what was going on in my house. Who knows what I stirred up by digging around in the attic? One thing at a time, though. Time to set things right with T.

There she was, waiting for me at the crossroads of Bay Breeze Way and Myrtle Lane like nothing had changed. Only she wasn't smiling at me. She was looking down at her shoes. Or her boots, rather. T had taken liberties with the traditional fall colors with this ensemble. She was wearing teal corduroy overalls with a black turtleneck—how she was going to survive in this get-up with our rising fall temps was beyond me. And those slouchy pleather boots she was looking at were a deep, dark purple, circa 1984, if I had to guess. Her look was topped off with her batty headband that she'd been sporting during spooky season since middle school. I got right in front of her, and she still wouldn't look up, not even offering a hello.

"Hey," I said, speaking first, cutting through the silence.

T glanced up at me, bats on springs wavering above her head. Her eyes were watery. Shit.

"Hey, hey T. I'm sorry. I was a total bitch the other day. I was just so shocked by the news about Kelly and all. I know it's no excuse. You're my friend, my best friend. I shouldn't have acted that way, shut you out.

And that was all it took. T lunged at me, hugging me tightly in one of her famous hugs. And I let her. I hugged her back, too.

T stepped back, wiping her eyes, quietly laughing. "It's okay. Yeah, sure, I was mad. I was hurt. But I *know* you. I know you needed time to work all this out. I had faith. You never have to go it alone, though. We are a team. You know that, right? Have you been able to see Kelly?"

As we walked to school, I let her in on what happened during my visit to the hospital and the shit that had been going down at home. Her eyes got big, and she froze for a second.

"Blink, T. Blink. Breathe," I said, shaking her gently by the shoulders.

"Oh gosh! I mean, holy shit! Do you think... do you think... *they're baaack?*"

Leave it to T to reference a classic 80s thriller like *Poltergeist.*

"Shit. I don't know, T. It all seems familiar, the cold spots, phantom fingers making contact with me, the feeling like I'm not alone. The one thing I know for sure is I am definitely getting Thing One and Thing Two to come over again with their ectoplasmic equipment and help me find out what the heck is going on."

"Are *they* baaack? I mean, I know a lot of people evacuated."

"I'm not sure. But I know that with most places opening back up, I bet I can find out. Maybe Bennie knows something. You know, she wasn't an original Woo Woo Girl, but she sure seems to have edged her way right into our full moon circle."

"Fer sure."

So, we were on an 80s kick, I gathered.

"Like totally," I added.

T snickered at this. It was like old times, like normal.

"Come on," I pleaded, "We don't want to be late. We better jam."

With a final "Bitchin," T grabbed my hand, giving it a gentle squeeze, and we just fell back in step, side by side.

I only had four classes this year. Math, English, advanced art, and another elective. I had chosen a digital design class. I thought it could only help with my art skills. I was still working on that self-portrait piece. I knew I needed to pick a focus. Maybe it would be design. I mean, it was senior year. I needed to start thinking about college. Shit. It was past time. I'd probably just end up taking my first year at the local community college. But maybe I still had time to decide? I'd probably end up majoring in art. Just something else for Mother to be pissed off about if she even knew what was what these days.

When I got to the shop, I was hit in the face with fall, the air steeped with the aroma of autumn, flavored coffee, pumpkin bread, pecan cinnamon rolls — a favorite from the island location. Yep. I'd definitely be taking one or two or three of those rolls to go home with me. There was soft jazz playing and there was Tristan behind the counter with her typical surly expression, looking beat. That was her norm.

"Hi," I said, kind of quietly.

"Hey," she shot back, blowing her bangs out of her face in a huff.

"How's it been going here?"

"Just fine. When I got here this morning, Bennie had been here for hours it seemed, giving the shop what it needed to bring in the seasonal change. I have to admit...it's...nice." She shot me a tight-faced grin and nodded, looking around the room at the fake fall foliage and the Halloween-ish decor.

It's nice? I don't think I'd ever heard Tristan say anything was "nice." This must be her happy face. I'd never seen it.

Then she added, "I'm going to take off now.

Go get my brood together. You got this?"

"Sure."

Grabbing her bag, she gently touched my shoulder and was gone.

Whoa. Was Tristan not only saying things were nice but was she also being nice to *me*? I had to let that sink in for a minute. Maybe the seasons weren't the only things that were shifting.

About that time, the front door opened and in walked Ro. She was wearing head to toe black, like some kind of skintight bodysuit with boots. Well, not quite head. On her head was a rust-colored beret, her nod to the season. It sat askew atop her black locks, the purple streaks now fading to lavender.

She walked up to the counter, her teeth tugging on her bottom lip. Damn.

I managed a weak "Uh, hi there."

"Hi yourself, Elia. Can I get a lavender latte with coconut milk to go?"

Was she going to be all business? Maybe I'd misread her signals the last time I saw her.

"Um, sure. Sure." Uh and um. My vocabulary was in top form today.

I turned around to begin her order and heard her start, "Even though school sucks, it was good to get back into class, don't cha think?"

"Yeah, yeah. Sure." I answered over my shoulder, steam rising from the espresso machine. My conversation skills, stimulating. *Geeze. Pull it together, Elia.*

"You going to the Harvest Dance next week? I mean, I know school dances are lame and all, but it is our senior year. Not much time left for *making memories and enjoying the teen years.* At least, that's what my mom says anyway. You know, they like to live through us vicariously, trying to recapture their youth."

I turned to give Ro her go cup. Again, with the "Yeah. Yeah. Sure." What was wrong with me? Ok. I knew what was wrong with me. It'd been too long. Too long since I'd liked anyone "that way." I was rusty.

Ro looked at me, puzzled. *"Elia, say something, anything,"* my inner voice was screaming at me now. "Yeah. I mean, yes. I'm going with a friend." Fuck. I didn't want to say *that.*

"Oh," was all she said back, her coffee

suddenly becoming very interesting. She pursed her lips, blowing on her drink, a little foam getting on her upper lip. Her tongue darted out slowly, licking away the milk.

"But. But. She, I mean T, is just a friend. I kind of promised her we'd go together. She's really into this, the dance, the clothes and all."

"Oh?" she said again, but there was a question in that reply hanging in the air.

"Yep, Yeah." I was back to one-word answers.

"Well, I'll see you there." And then, she was leaving.

Quick, say something, something clever, something sexy, the voice in my head commanding me. I could hear my heart beating in my ears. I was sweating, definitely sweating. I started to tell her something, wanting to say anything that wasn't monosyllabic before she left. And just then, she stopped, came back to the counter, and motioned to me with one finger while leaning over, her chest resting on the counter. I leaned in, her mouth now so close to my cheek I could feel her breath, and she whispered, "By the way, I'm going commando."

Then, her hand covered mine as she stared deep into my eyes, a toothy smile spreading across her face, one side tilting upwards, her eyebrows raised, up and down, and up and down. I was left standing there agog, my inner voice now saying, *What the…? How…how did she know?*

~*~

And in the blink of an eye, the day of the dance was here. And it wasn't the only thing that was here. Halloween had come in full force to our little coastal town. Ghosts were hanging from trees, tombstones lined yards, a scary clown here, a lone red balloon there. Some had even set out "Caution" tape over fallen fences and upturned trees, stumps and gnarly roots, earth exposed from the last storm, people making do in the in-between. It was festive, and I couldn't help smiling. This was a me I didn't recognize. The me that was softening, letting in the light.

There was T, meeting me out in front of my house on the sidewalk, looking like the harvest queen in a long white peasant dress with an empire waist, her rib cage cinched in gold braid, and cleavage. Where had T been hiding that cleavage?

Her ginger hair was encircled with flowers and leaves, and her makeup—T had gone all out—her makeup simple, light, but with her lashes long and jet black, gold glitter, heavy, framing her face. She looked amazing.

We hugged. I needed my daily T hug, but these days, I was giving as good as I got. I stepped back and did a slow twirl, showing off my latest thrift store find. I was still in black, but I was glittering myself. I had on a 70s sequined halter maxi dress, and tucking my hair behind my ears, I let my rhinestone earrings dance in the streetlamp light. Then, I hiked up my hem, showing off my shabby Docs. We both snickered at this!

T brought her hands together, slowly, over and over and over in dramatic applause. Then, she said, "Not bad. Not bad at all. Now, back in the house, missy. You need makeup." I just sighed and linked my arm in hers as we headed into my house.

Up in my bathroom, *the* bathroom, T began to use my face as her canvas.

"Crap, Elia. It's freaking freezing in here."

"I know. I know. I've been doing the stuff

the twins suggested, putting out stuff at night for Aunt Laera, but…"

"What the what? Oh right. I'd happily forgotten about all that, Elia. Ok. Ok. Now, fast version of a makeover."

T let out a long exhale and sped up her handiwork. Ten minutes hadn't passed when she said, "Now, there."

I looked at myself in the mirror. Damn. I looked good! "How, how did you do that so fast, T?"

"Well, we have been friends for years, Elia. You just needed something to bring out your blue eyes and accent your Clara Bow lips."

I didn't know who the hell Clara Bow was, but then again, I wasn't as into this girly stuff as much as T was. She'd lined my eyes in kohl, dragging out the ends in a wing-ed cat eye, and painted my lips burgundy.

"Just a little powder to set your face, and, there. All done. Now, let's get the heck out of this meat locker. I'm not in the mood to see any of your family."

I gave T a hug in thanks. She looked a little

surprised, but I was trying. Then, we were back on the sidewalk, heading to the school as night crept in. I felt a slight breeze and something like hands trying to grip my shoulders, pulling me back, and then nothing. Whatever or whoever that was, let go.

The dance was in the gym, but the space had been completely transformed. It wasn't dark and spooky like I'd imagined. It was...bright. It looked like a scene from Ari Aster's *Midsommar*. I liked an A24 film as much as anybody else, but so much light...for the harvest dance? Long tables flanked the room covered in white cloths. Boughs of multicolored flowers hung from the rafters. As I was feeling disappointed, I looked over at T and her face was happy, shining. I wasn't going to spoil her mood.

"Oh. Oh!" she exclaimed. "It's not what I thought it would look like, but oh!"

Then, I noticed in the back corner a yellow A-frame structure and what seemed to be a bear? For photos? I guess someone had embraced the whole movie theme thing, but I felt they'd gotten their equinoxes screwed up or something.

I was just about to mention this to T when I saw her. There she was, Ro. She had on a dress similar to T's, but it was red. A deep red satin, the color of blood. And instead of a gold braid, her torso was corseted with black rope. And her purple streaks were now crimson, hair was in a multitude of tiny braids festooned with long, black ribbons. She looked like one of Dracula's brides, and I was shook. And then, she looked at me, her eyes a flame.

She walked over to us, and I could feel the air change. T took a tiny step back.

"Wow! Hey." I was back to my cavegirl speak. And that's all I could say. What felt like a half an hour passed, but I'm sure it was only seconds, I came back to my senses. "Uh, Ro, hey. This is my *friend*, T." I reached behind me and pulled T next to me.

"Hi T," Ro extended her hand, and T took it.

"I recognize you from the sidewalk, eh, I mean *BB's*," T said nervously, shaking her hand and quickly dropping it.

Me. Still tongue-tied. Ro spoke next. "Elia, do you want to dance?"

And just as I was about to say, "But, there's no..." the bright lights were turned off, and the gym was alit like a fairy garden all in soft white twinkling lights. And then, music. Magic.

"I...I'm going...to get a drink...ok, Elia?" T stammered as she put her hand on my arm, checking to see if I was ok.

"Yes, Ok. Fine." I'd found three words. These words floated into the air, barely reaching T as Ro led me out onto the floor.

She pulled me in tight, hip to hip, never breaking eye contact with me. Her nails scraped my arms, up and down. I thought, I thought she might kiss me right there in the middle of it all. The air was thick, I could barely move. I sure as shit couldn't speak. I felt...I felt light and heavy at the same time, a warmth spreading over my whole body, and my legs were weak. This was a different kind of magic. Her face close to mine, she pulled me even closer, then turning, she rested her chin on my shoulder. I swallowed hard and tried to breathe normally as we swayed. And then I saw them across the room — The Satanic Six, well, Five right now. And Doc was watching us, watching me, and smiling a psychotic smile that I'd seen before. These were another group of Horrifying Women, flesh and blood, live and in person. I forgot that Ro was a part of them. Looking at them, I tried to relax. I put my head on Ro's shoulder and shut my eyes. It was then I smelled it, the pungent aroma of cloves. She reeked of it.

CHAPTER 8

THEN

It's dark. I'm in a cramped space, fumbling around, trying to find an opening, an exit. Where am I? What is this memory? Am I locked in the closet with the rats? Is it the night that Mom locked me away in the dark to help me see the light? Or is it the night when I was at T's, spell work gone wrong? Lying on the floor, my ankle sliced and bleeding, the lights outed seemingly by a gust of air that came out of nowhere.

In my stupor, I reach down, touching my ankle. No. No fresh blood. My fingers traced what was just a scar. A scar formed over a wound created by some unseen force and, well, by my own hand. No. This place. This space it's not either of those times. Still grappling, images begin to form in front of me, faces. I can't make them out. They come in and out of focus. And then, I see! It's not my ancestors, not the OG Horrifying Women, but The Six, well, The Five. And I'm dancing with Ro, trying hard, so hard to focus on the pleasure and not the what ifs. I'm trying to forget that Ro is part of The Six. Is it Then or Now. I feel so confused... like I've been spelled.

NOW

Shit. It was a dream. Some fucked up vision, all mashed up with the past and the present. Residue in my brain leftover from the night before. I sat up in bed. Oof. I laid back down, my head flopping onto the pillow but not before I caught a glimpse of an overturned wine bottle on my bedroom floor. Oh fuck. Had I drunk an entire bottle last night?

Ok. Ok. I lay there in a t-shirt damp with sweat and my Saturday panties. At least I'd made an effort to get the day right for the dance and gotten out of my dress before I'd passed out. The Harvest Dance. Ok. Think back, Elia. I remember meeting T and walking into the gym. I remember seeing Ro in all of her striking, vampire-like glory. Goddess, she was hot. Then, we were dancing, and I saw them, The Six, no, The Five. I wanted to trust Ro so badly I forgot she came with *them.* Or I wanted to forget anyway. What she stirred in me…I was thinking below my waist and not with my head.

In my hungover state, I realized my hand had slipped between my thighs with thoughts of Ro. I stopped myself. I needed to do *that*, yes, but I also needed to get cleaned up and get rid of this fuck all headache. Before I left my room, I looked over at my desk and my own personal pharmacy, trying to remember if I'd taken my meds last night. It wasn't good to skip the daily dose, but was it worse to wash them down with what was equal to about 5 glasses of vino? The "something like lavender" which I was *supposed* to take every day was knocked over, top off, capsules strewn about. Maybe that meant I'd taken them. I was getting into some bad habits. Maybe at least I was remembering to take the good with the bad?

Bathroom light on, ugh. I looked in the mirror. Geeze. What a sight! I saw the glass of wine I'd left out for Aunt Laera. I'd remembered the ritual, but the glass remained full. What did that mean? I didn't know enough about this spirit stuff or hauntings. Was this a haunting? I had freaking ghosts in my house; I'd just never said the word out loud before, haunting. I needed more information. Make a mental note, Elia. Contact Mary and try to find The Ghostly Gals and see if they were back in town.

I looked at myself again, grimaced, reached for the pain meds, and downed the leftover wine, hair of the dog, wishing away the pain in my skull. Filling the bath with water as hot as I could stand it, I stepped in and submerged myself in the tub's depths, staring through the steam at nothing in particular. I dunked myself, soaped up, and then sat in the now cloudy water, letting the yuck of the night before wash away.

Pushing away the bad stuff, I let myself relive the good stuff. I remember what it felt like, dancing Ro, her hands stroking my arms, then finding my waist. Our hips, our girl parts, pressed against each other. My hand had found its way again to the place where my legs met. I stopped myself. I wanted more. I let some of the water out, turned the water back on, testing the temperature, not too hot, not too cold. Then, I slid myself down to the end of the tub positioning myself under the faucet, legs up the wall. I closed my eyes, letting my head drop back, and used my hands to lift my hips. I let the water run down and over me.

I moved my body up and down and side to side. I was close. My lips parted, and I was taking in short gasps of air when something changed. The water felt weird. Stringy. I lifted my head and opened my eyes. Hair. Grey, greasy threads were pouring out of the faucet. I screamed, scrambling, finding myself upright, turning and turning the hot and cold dials. They felt stripped. Then, they began to spin on their own! I watched for a second, the knobs going round and round furiously and hair, more and more of it now forming some kind of nasty puddle near the drain. And then...and then...one, no, two fingers began to emerge from the opening. I just stared, frozen, looking at the two long, arthritic digits, knobby knuckles, the flesh a yellowish pink, the nails caked with what looked like soil. And the smell of something rotting. I snapped to my senses and began to back away, slipping one foot and then the other. I couldn't get any traction. Like they had a life of their own, the strands on the tub floor wound around themselves, becoming rope-like and like tentacles, wrapping around my ankles, my legs, dragging me towards the drain, towards the fingers.

I screamed again, but no sound was coming out — just nothing but strained muscles, my mouth, my throat, my body — everything tight, constricted, immobile. I couldn't breathe. Then, everything went dark. After what seemed like an hour, the lights came back on. I knew it couldn't have been that long. It just felt like it. I was sitting in the tub, naked, damp, and shivering. I leaned over the side and vomited onto the floor, wine, water, and... and...hair, gobs and gobs of hair spilling out onto the tiles into a foul, disgusting heap.

~*~

On Monday, I met T in front of the school. I'd spent the rest of Sunday in slow motion, trying to feel better and cleaning up the God-awful mess in my bathroom. It wasn't easy in my hungover state. I'd wipe up some of the puke, start to retch, and puke again in the puke. It was a long freaking day.

I didn't know what to expect from T. I'd acted like an ass again, ditching her at the dance. I don't remember everything from that night except for walking home alone. That and dancing with Ro. That much I remembered. There she was, festooned in the shades of the season. Her headpiece from Saturday night was reimagined, just with fall foliage now, crowing her head. The rest of her was covered in a peach-colored fuzzy sweater dress, her look finished off with dark green leg warmers over chocolate suede boots. I wanted to run and hug her and have a tactile experience. She looked like a pile of freshly raked leaves, but she probably felt like a cozy blanket on a crisp day, and I wanted to wrap myself up and be comforted. The other night, though, I'd pushed the limits of our friendship yet again, so I kept my distance.

She spoke first. "So…how did it go the other night?" Her expression—not what I expected—that of a Cheshire cat, grinning slyly.

What? She was fishing for info. She wasn't mad. Ok. I could work with this. Maybe this was one of those girl situations—let's pretend like nothing happened, sweep it under the rug situations.

"Well…T. I'll tell you. It's been a hot minute since I've felt anything like this. A long damn time." And, I began to relay what it was like, the feelings, being close to Ro. I kind of fudged and glossed over the rest of the weekend, like my hangover and the nasty "visitation." The attack, in this version, became a migraine and a relaxing soak. I didn't want to freak her out.

T beamed at me, her eyes alight with mischief. "Now what?" she wondered aloud.

"Well…I don't know. Like I said, it's been a while. I'm not sure how to proceed. What do you think?" I knew T lived for this kind of shit, and she'd have all the answers.

"Ask her out. Tell her I'm coming over too. Saturday night, for a movie night, the late-night spook fest of films. Then, I'll just mysteriously fall ill," she said, placing the back of her hand on her forehead as though she had the vapors. "And you and Ro can have the night all to yourselves." I have to admit, it was a good plan. She giggled, giving me a quick hug. Then, she pulled back. "But… what about…*the others*?"

The others? At first, I thought she meant the ghosts, but I realized she meant The Six or The Five. "I don't know, T. She doesn't seem like the rest of them. I *want* to be able to trust her. Part of my growth, you know?" T just nodded.

"I'll feel her out Saturday. Get an idea of what her part in their group is. See if she's her own person."

"Oh. Ok. You *feel* her out. And then, I want ALL of the details, k?"

"Ok. Yeah. I get it." I got it. And I wanted to get more this weekend.

~*~

It wasn't hard. I waited a couple of days after passing Ro in the halls, exchanging side-long glances. And then, I just did it, I walked up to her, asking her over to hang out with me and T. And she said yes. Now, I just had to wait.

Over the next few days I cleaned, now past my queasiness. I religiously took my meds, and I did the nightly ritual. The wine glass was now empty each morning, and things seemed to be back on track. I knew I was playing with the woo, not knowing enough but doing what I'd been told.

Dealing with the experts would have to wait. I'd called Mary and the twins weren't back in town yet. Talking to Mary, I let my thoughts drift back to Kelly. Kelly. I thought about her in the quiet moments. I had to try to get back over to the hospital. Mary had said she still hadn't been able to see her, but at least the nurses had relaxed a little and let her peek into the small window in the door. Mary said she seemed stable.

Saturday, T began to text.

OMG. 2nite is the nite! R U redy?

Yup yup. House clean. All set. Nerves tho.

U got this! K?

K. K.

2morrow I want deets. Gud luck

Thx

About 10 pm, Ro was at my front door. I'd texted her my address. I looked out of the window. She had on that catsuit she'd been wearing in the shop that one day. The day she had told me she was going commando. I'd forgotten about that. How the fuck did she know about the underwear game? Telling me something like that wasn't *too* unbelievable. T and I couldn't be the only people in the world to play it, right? At any rate, I'd put on good underwear tonight, just in case we were up to playing our own games.

"Hi," Ro said, looking up at me from under her black bangs with those eyes, more green tonight than yellow, the smell of lavender coming off of her skin.

"Hi, yourself," and...I just stood there, staring right back at her.

"Well...are you going to invite me in?"

"Oh, yeah. Sorry. Sure. Welcome, walk this way, ah, ah, ah." I said, mimicking the voice of The Count on *Sesame Street*. I wanted to disappear below the floor.

"K," she said looking past me into the living room, "Where's T?"

"Oh, she can't make it. Not feeling great. Maybe the flu?" I was improvising somewhat. I'd have to get my story straight with T later, just in case.

"Oh. The flu. That's...too bad. It's just you and me, huh?"

"Yep. Yep. So...want a tour?"

"Yes, please. It's just you here. You get to live by yourself?"

"Yep. I get to live all by myself." No mention of the occasional visitors.

I began to take Ro around the house, stopping first in the kitchen, pouring a glass of wine, and cutting a piece of rosemary before heading upstairs. Shit, I nicked my finger with the scissors. I quickly wrapped a paper towel around my index finger.

"Uh. What's that for?"

"This? Oh, it's just something I do every night, like...like a ritual?"

I left it as a question, testing the waters.

"You mean, like putting up protection... like...from ghosts?"

"Something like that."

Ok. So, she was into it. I told her about Aunt Laera and The Horrifying Women. I told her *some* of it, including going to the gatherings with the Woo Woo Girls, but I left a lot out on purpose. I didn't want to seem like too much of a freak.

We went up to the bathroom and I showed her what I did each night. Then, we headed into my bedroom.

"Purple, cool. I like it. So...what are we going to watch? And...where..."

"I'm thinking the 1979 version, *Dracula* with

Frank Langella. You game? And as far as where…
on…my bed?" I again left it with a question.

With that, Ro pounced, landing in the center
of my bed. Question answered.

But…overthinking things, instead of acting,
I decided to broach the subject of The Six.

"Ro, let me ask you something." She looked
at me, waiting. "I want to know more about your
group, your friends, you know, the girls you hang
out with most of the time, outside the coffee shop,
Doc and them?"

"Doc? Oh, you mean Luna. You know,
you're not the only one who calls her that. I don't
know why everybody thinks she's a dealer."

She was laughing at this. Maybe things
weren't at all like they seemed. Maybe T and I
were just being judgy.

Since she seemed to be in a light mood, I
went on, telling her how T and I called them The
Satanic Six, sharing the nick names we'd come up
with for them, including the one for her, Oh Joy.
Now, she was really laughing. In fact, she almost
fell off my bed.

"Oh. My. God," she said, trying to catch her

breath. "You guys are *too* funny!" Then she went on, and I learned all of their real names. I knew her name, of course, short for Aurora, and now Doc was Luna? I was going to have to get that one straight in my head. Then let's see, Bitchy was Ava (*so* did not fit her), Mouse was Penny. Couch was Elizabeth or Ebeth, and Cola was Jo Jo.

"Wait. Wait, Elia. I get most of these, but Cola? Where the heck did you come up with that one?"

"She's always sneezing, wiping her nose on her sleeve. T and I thought maybe she had a coke problem."

"Oh shit!" She was losing it again in a giggle fit. "Oh shit, Elia. Jo Jo has *major* allergies. She even has an inhaler."

"Oh," was all I could say, feeling kind of stupid. I was back to my elegant vocab.

"Now, Elia. They're just my friends. Luna, well she does have a chip on her shoulder. And Ava, too. They don't have the best home lives. Dads are AWOL. And their moms…well…let's just say they aren't storybook moms, you know?"

"Oh." I knew all too well. And I said as much.

But that was all I said. No question left hanging in the air. I ended *that* with a definite period. Not going to let all my crazy out too soon and scare her off.

"You know," she said, "We have gatherings of our own. You should totally come sometime."

"You do? I mean, Y'all do too? What kind of gatherings?"

"A little of this, a little of that...you know, magic shit."

"Ah. Well, yeah. What with *Blue* damaged from the hurricane and most of my group out of town and Kelly…" My voice dropped out with the mention of Kelly. But I swallowed hard and stuffed my feelings down. I didn't want to put a damper on the night. "Yeah. Sounds like fun. When do you meet next?"

"Well on Samhain, you big dope. Don't cha know? It's one of the best nights to work spells. The veil is thin," she added, wiggling her woo woo fingers in the air in front of my face.

"Oh yeah. Cool. I'm in!"

"Yeah, cool. You'll make us 7. Lucky number 7."

Hmm. I thought about that, but only for a second. I *did* feel lucky, heh heh, and with my apprehension pacified, I grabbed my laptop, plopped down next to Ro, and pushed PLAY.

CHAPTER 9

I laid around by myself on Sunday, streamed a couple of shows, ghost hunting types, looking for information. Everything seemed back to normal. The wine in the bathroom was disappearing again at night and there were no more empty glasses or bottles in my room for that matter. I was doing good. I could still smell her in my bed. Not cloves, but lavender.

I was doing more than good. Last night was… damn good. Ro had stayed late. We finished the vampire flick and then talked for hours. Holding hands, our legs entwined as we faced each other. Just. Talking. I thought for sure that she'd kiss me but it wasn't until she was leaving that she leaned in and placed her lips lightly on my cheek. On my cheek. Was I reading all of this wrong? I needed to get feedback from T. I was about to have to rehash all of this anyway. There was no way T would stand for anything less. She'd want information.

Monday morning, I was out the door and ran smack into T. She looked electric in a neon top with leg warmers to match and a leopard print mini, and today, cat ears. She was literally jumping up and down, about to come out of her own skin.

"Oh hey! Ok. Ok. I was too, too excited. I couldn't wait to meet at our usual spot. Now, spill it!"

I started to tell her all about Saturday night, from when Ro got there until she left hours later. T looked...disappointed, like someone had let the starch out of her.

"What?" I asked.

"Well, nothing. I just thought...maybe something *else* had happened, you know... something juicier?"

"Ew."

"Uh...gross, you know what I mean. So, nothing?"

I just shook my head slowly from side to side.

"T, do you think I'm creating all of this in my head, like, I'm imagining it all?"

"No, Elia. I don't think so. But..."

"But what?"

"The part about the *others*. Are you sure you

want to get involved with *that*?"

"Oh, T. I'm sure it's fine. I can handle them. She comes with *them* so…"

"Speaking of handle," and T grabbed my hand, inspecting it, turning it this way and that. "What's this? A small cut. You…ok?"

I knew what she meant. T didn't mean was I physically ok, but mentally. She knew about my tendencies. I hadn't even thought about snipping my finger until just now.

"No. I mean, yeah. I'm ok. I'm fine. I'm just fine."

"Okay. Good. We better motor then." She winked, gave me a quick squeeze, and began to roll down the sidewalk. My Goddess, she was wearing Heelys.

Quickly shutting the door, I had to break into a small run just to catch up with her. When I did, we smiled at each other and then were silent the rest of the way to school. Sometimes, we didn't need words. Our friendship had that kind of familiar ease. Gave me time to think. Like, I was thinking, *Ok. Maybe I wasn't inventing a relationship with Ro. Maybe she did like me in that way. Another*

gathering of magical girls would be cool to check out.
And, and I picked up the house yesterday. What the hell
had happened to that bloody napkin that I'd used to blot
my cut Saturday night?

I'd seen Ro in the halls at school with The Six always in a huddle. She smiled at me a few times, and I feebly waved back. Doc/Luna smirking at me every time. Every. Fucking. Time. This went on for a couple of days. Finally, she came up to me alone.

"Hey."

"Hey, yourself." Okay, I was a little pissed.

"You ok, Elia?"

"Yeah. It's been a few days. I just thought…"

Ugh. I was acting needy. This was definitely *not* a turn-on.

"Yeah, right, it's *only* been a few days."

Ro had closed the gap between us and was stroking my arm, consoling me. I felt like a loser with a capital "L."

I tried to brush it off. "Sure. No. You're right." I was back to my sparkling conversation.

She'd stopped stroking my arm. Now, she had me by the hand, her nails grazing my upturned palm. That was the move. I felt it in my knees.

"Well…It's only five days 'til Samhain. You still going to meet with me and the girls or The Satanic Six as you say?" She was smiling and biting her lower lip at the same time.

"Oh. Yeah. Yes." I am a robot. I speak words.

Ro leaned in and quickly kissed me on the cheek. "Great! I'll text you with the deets. Oh. There is one thing. I hope you don't think it's too weird, but when we work spells, we use blood… as an offering, you know, makes the magic stronger."

Yeah, I knew all about *that*, and I can't say I was too thrilled about the request. When I didn't say anything, she started again.

"Oh no. Don't freak out on me. It's cool if that's too much for you. We were all looking forward to you joining us. We've been looking for a seventh sister for a while now. Penny could sense something about you, a strength. She has a gift for that. We really *need* you in our circle."

Penny…oh…Mouse. Apparently, Penny/Mouse was clairsentient, if that was the correct terminology that I remembered Kelly telling me. Kelly. What would she think about all this? Would she trust them? I should try to go see her this week, see if I can get in. Maybe *I* can sense something.

"No. I mean, yeah. I'm in. So, yeah, just shoot me the info, and I'll be there. Oh. By the way, what or…how do you all include the blood in your work?"

"Oh, that." She ran her pointed nails through her mane, giving her hair a tousle. "We use our period blood. Just try to get a sample in a little container and bring it with you. That's all, ya big dope." She winked at me and walked off.

Oh. That's all.

I turned around, and T popped out from behind the lockers. Her eyes and mouth wide open. Shit. She was just standing there, not saying a word. Then, she took her hand and placed it under her chin, closing her gaping mouth.

"Oh. Hey T," I said, my voice cracking a bit.

Still, she said nothing.

"I…I was just catching up with Ro."

"Uh, no, that's not all you were doing. I heard *everything*."

Oh crud. Now, it was my turn to be silent.

"Elia, what the heck are you thinking?

Wasn't the stuff that went down over the summer enough for you, enough to let you know *not* to mess with the dark shit? Blood? Blood! You know what happened over the summer. And you know, it's not just the dark magic. It's, it's, you know."

Yes, I knew exactly what she meant. My triggers. My coping skills. I tried to reassure her.

"Look, T, it's all cool. It'll be fine, just fine." Mentally, I saw a house bursting into flames. Yeah, fine.

"I know we're getting older, Elia, and I can't tell you what to do. Just, just be careful, ok?"

"You want me to see if you can come too?"

T let out a burst of forced air between her lips. "Ah, no. No thanks, Elia. Just, just text me if you need me for anything, k?"

"I will. Geeze. Don't worry. It will all be fine. Just fine." Now, I didn't see a house exploding. I saw red, deep red. Something dark, like death.

I needed to see Kelly. I needed to figure out if I was doing the right thing. I'd told T everything was fine, but honestly, I didn't know what the hell I was doing. Even if Kelly couldn't say anything to me, maybe, maybe, I'd get some kind of sign.

~*~

After calling Mary, we met on the first floor of the hospital. She said nothing to me, just pulled me in for a quick hug. Into the elevator and stepping out to the floor of intensive care. We were walking straight towards Kelly's room and were just reaching the door when that nurse stopped us, pinching me on my elbow.

"Ok. You two. I recognize you both. I *know* neither of you are family. I can't let either of you in for a visit."

Mary started to say something, but before she could, I turned on the tears. "Miss, you just gotta let us at least look in on her. My mom's away, not doing well, and this lady right here and Kelly are just about all of the family I have in town." Then, one big teardrop escaped the corner of my eye and traced a wet line down the side of my face.

Nursey-nurse huffed, rolled her eyes, and put her hands on her hips. "Ok. There is no way I can let you in the room, but I'm not going to say anything if you two just stand out here and peep in for, let's say, 5 minutes or so. Ok?"

My face lit up, and Mary smiled softly and

mouthed a "thank you" to nursey-nurse. We stood there, side by side, taking turns looking in. It was not good. Her jet-black hair, now lighter at the roots, looked slick with sweat. And I thought maybe by now her bruising would have started to fade, but it looked even worse. Her skin was terribly discolored, the tattoo on her left forearm hardly visible. Mary put her head down and put one hand up to that small, glass window, sending her love and energy perhaps. I just took short, shallow breaths, trying to steady myself. What was going to happen to her? It didn't seem like any family had come in to check on her. What could we do, the Woo Woo Girls? We weren't blood. I felt hopeless.

I looked back at the nurse's station, and that nurse was tapping her watch and looking at me and Mary. I tugged on Mary's sleeve and gestured with my head towards the elevators. We were quiet on the ride down until we were outside of the hospital.

"What can we do, Mary? How can we help her? Doesn't she have any relatives?"

"I'm not sure, Elia. I feel like all we can do in

the short term is pray, send healing energy. Keep hoping the nursing staff will let us in eventually."

"I feel...I feel...powerless."

"Oh, Elia, you are far from powerless. Get still. Breathe. Look inside. You'll find the answers there. Goddess will speak to you in those moments. I do have to say, though, you don't seem completely yourself lately. I know there's been a lot going on, the storm and everything..."

I lied. I was off kilter, and I didn't want to get into my craziness at the moment, the new love interest, The Six, the return of the ghosts, the wine...my meds... "Oh, no, Mary. I'm fine. Just fine." That was becoming my mantra, apparently.

"Good, good. Now, I've got to fly. I've got to find out when the other gals are coming back to town. It's almost Samhain, you know. We've got to find a place to gather. Are you and T going to meet with us?"

I knew that was what I *should* do. I needed the gals. I needed to get in touch with the ghostologists, but there was Ro...

"Um, I'm not sure. Let me text T and see what's up, k? I know we're a little old for Trick or

Treat, but still…"

"Sure. I understand. I forgot it's Halloween, too. We'll be waiting to hear from you. Take care, sweetie."

I just smiled and nodded, my head bobbing along. Then, I started to walk home. I was up in my thoughts, the sides of my brain in a tug-o-war. Should I do this *or* that? Of course, my hormones would rule. Of course, I'd go with Ro and The Six. As I drew closer to home, I felt the icy fingers reaching for me, only they had me by the neck this time, pulling me home. I tried to shake it off. Inside, I snipped the rosemary and poured the wine, too. I dutifully left the glass and the herbs in the bathroom for Aunt Laera. Then, once in my room, I popped my "something for sleep" capsules and lay there, within my purple walls, staring at the ceiling, wondering where I was in my cycle and thinking, "*How in the hell was I going to capture my period blood in five days?*"

CHAPTER 10

It was Halloween. Or Samhain for some. There wouldn't be a full moon gathering, but the Girls would be meeting in Mary's home for the sabbat. The Girls were more Goddess-loving than witchy or Wiccan, but they still recognized the turning of the wheel. I'd been texting T. She'd been kind of ghosting me lately, which wasn't like her at all. From the looks of things, she wasn't interested in hanging out, staying up late, or watching crappy, old scary movies as was the usual on this night. The midnight *Rocky Horror Picture Show* was out, too. Anyway, I'd be heading out to meet Ro soon, and then we'd join The Five, er Six, no, we were The Seven now. Hi ho.

I'd gotten "the stuff." Luckily, I'd started just a couple of days ago, and days two and three were really heavy and crampy for me, so it wasn't hard. I just sat on the toilet and held a glass jar between my legs, and drip, drip, drip. Eww. I hoped it was enough.

Ro would be here soon, so I slipped on one of

my loose-fitting, long, black secondhand dresses —
totally bloated — and put on my Docs. She was at
the front door, wearing her tight black body suit
yet again. I wasn't complaining.

"Hey there," she said, leaning in and giving
me a peck on the cheek. "You got everything for
tonight?"

"Yep," I said, patting my bag. I really needed
to work on my conversation skills.

"Great! The others are sooo excited you're
coming. I can't wait for you to join in, see what we
do."

She held my hand, and we started to walk
down the sidewalk. I didn't feel the ghosts tonight,
which was weird because it was Samhain, and
the veil was supposed to be thin. I didn't give it
another thought, though. It was nice to have her
fingers entwined with mine.

"Luna doesn't live far. We're gonna circle
up in her attic tonight," She said, waving woo woo
fingers in my face with her other hand.

"Cool." Cool? Come on, Elia. You can do
better than that. "I mean. Awesome. Looking
forward to it." Try harder, Elia. "I mean, I only

have experience with the Girls and doing some spell work with T, so, yeah, it's cool, I wanna see what y'all do."

Ro just smiled at me, pulling me along. "We're here!"

What? We turned the corner onto Dogwood Trace. Luna lived *that* close to me, like only one street over?

"Wow. Fast." Must speak more words. "Cool." Again, with the cool. I wasn't feeling very sure of myself hooking up with this new group. And my heart hurt. I was thinking about Kelly, T, and the other Girls. I let out an exhale through closed lips, making a sound like a leaky balloon.

"What the hell was that?" Ro was laughing at me now.

"Nothing, nothing, just breathing, thinking."

"C'mon. It's time!" There was that sparkling smile again. She gave my hand a quick squeeze for reassurance and then dropped it.

Luna's house was not like mine or T's. It was definitely not your typical Southern home. Everything was white, the walls, the furniture. On the walls hung black and white photography. No throw pillows or family photos anywhere. Very un-Southern.

Ro saw me taking it all in. "It's great, huh? Luna's mom is a decorator. So clean, minimalist, high-end, you know? She's out tonight with Ava's mom at some costume party at the country club, so we've got the whole house to ourselves!"

Cold. I was thinking cold. "Yeah, it's great. That's great." Cold.

Up three flights of floating stairs and we were at the attic door. Going in, squeals and giggles erupted. They were all there: Bitchy/Ava, Mouse/Penny, Couch/Ebeth, and Cola/Jo Jo. And in the back, smoking a clove cigarette, was Doc/Luna. Shooting daggers at me. Oh Joy, er Ro began to squeal too (the hell?), all of them jumping up and down, hugging me. Me trying to let them. All of them except Luna. I was here with The Satanic Six, and I couldn't believe it.

"We're so, sooo glad you're here!" Cola/Jo Jo practically screamed. Couch/Ebeth was nodding up and down and up and down in agreement like some deranged bobblehead.

"So, so glad," Bitchy/Ava added in her

deep, monotone way.

"I just knew you'd be a fit for us," Mouse/ Penny had joined in. "There's something about you, Elia. Something special. Something *powerful.*

I just looked back at her, my eyes wide in surprise, pulling my head back and straightening my spine. She must be joking, right? About that time, Ro took my hand again, trying to let me know everything was ok.

Luna put out her cigarette and sauntered over, taking long, slow steps. The rest of them parted, letting her through.

"Yes, yes. There *is* something about Elia, isn't there?" Luna said, cupping the side of my face with her perfectly manicured hand. "That makes us seven tonight. And *seven* is just what we need. Come, Elia. Join us."

With that, they all walked to the center of the room and made a circle around a pentagram someone had chalked out on the floor.

"Yes, seven is just what we need," Luna continued. "I know it's Samhain, and I know the veil is thin, and we could pull out the Ouija board and shit, but...the moon *is* waning. It's the purrfect time to do a ridding spell. And I have one in mind. It calls for seven, like the seven sisters of the underworld. You up for a ridding spell, Elia? Need to let go of anything? We sure are! We're ready to cut, cut, cut."

THEN

Cut, cut, cut. Did Luna know about my history? My mind went back to that night in the summer, the night in T's room when we'd first attempted our own ridding spell work. I remembered how T had so lovingly set up her room to look as much like *Blue* as it could. I remembered having Mom's writing, her shears. I'd been nervous, unsteady. I'd let go of the scissors at the same time a breeze came out of nowhere. Something or someone had interrupted our work. The gust somehow lifted the shears into the air. Then, down, down, down, they came, slicing my ankle open. Then, everything had gone dark until I came to in T's room, and she and Kelly were there beside me to make everything better. Kelly.

NOW

"Hey, hey! Are you ok?" It was Ro now, patting my face softly and shaking my shoulders. I'd fainted.

"Uh, yeah. I'm ok. Geez, I don't know what happened. Maybe I didn't eat enough today. Sorry to scare y'all." I feebly tried to push myself up off the floor.

"OMG, Elia! You scared the poo out of us! I thought you'd taken something, doped yourself up. You gave us quite a fright!" Mouse/Penny was helping me up now. The rest of The Six were nodding along. All except Luna. She just stood over me, her arms folded across her chest, smirking.

Luna sneered at me. "Well, if we're done with the drama now, let's get started."

And as Luna walked over to the pentagram, I noticed she was wearing a long cat's tail. Wait, were they all dressed up? Bitchy/Ava had on what, a fox tail? And Couch/Ebeth and Cola/Jo Jo had some kind of wings on their backs. I realized that they all had some sort of costume on. As Mouse/Penny put on bunny ears, she walked away, her back to me, hips swaying this way and that, a fluffy, cotton tail wiggled along with her. Had they done this while I'd been passed out or had they had this stuff on the whole time? I looked over at Ro, nothing but her form-fitting catsuit. A catsuit? I was beginning to feel like maybe I *was* doped up.

"Now, let's begin. Does everyone have their "blood" offering?" Luna's eyes were darting around the circle now, looking from one girl to the next. They all nodded en masse now and held out their jars and containers. I got mine out of my bag and quickly stepped back into my place in the circle.

"Elia, good, you brought yours too," Luna said, taking my jar and opening it. "Wait, the hell?" she said. "Is this *real* blood?"

"OMG, Elia," Mouse/Penny piped up. "We never use *real* blood. Ga-ross!"

I looked at Ro, and she just grinned sheepishly at me. Oh shit. I felt like a fool. I could have sworn Ro said to get my period blood. She did, didn't she? By now, they were all laughing. I felt like Sissy Spacek in *Carrie*. "They're all going to laugh at you..."

Luna composed herself. "No, no," she said, still stifling her laughter. I noticed her cat ears now — what the hell? "It's fine. It's good, Elia, really. You know as well as I do that *real* blood intensifies any magical working, right, Elia?"

Why was Luna directing so much personal stuff at me? Did she know about the stuff that went down over the summer? How could she?

"No sweat," I said. "Yeah, I know that. So, let's get started already." I tried to brush off my embarrassment and pull myself together. I was also trying not to think about Ro at the moment. Was she into me at all? What game was she playing?

"Good. It's time," Luna said as she moved into the center of the circle. Everyone again had their containers jutting out in front of them, silent, heads bowed. Luna moved from person to person, taking their "blood" and marking their foreheads with sigils. When she got to me, I straightened up, opened my jar, and not so gently shoved it out towards Luna, my eyes meeting hers and my mouth set tight, daring her. She reached two fingers in, dipping them in my blood, and drew a sign on my brow as well. Then, she dragged her fingertips down my throat and marked my chest as well, all the while never breaking eye contact. We were at some kind of standoff.

Luna sidled over to what I assumed was the head of the circle directly across from me, still staring at me. Then, she broke her gaze, closed her eyes, and raised her hand to the ceiling.

Addressing the group, Luna began to speak, "Does everyone have something in mind that they want to get rid of, something that is no longer serving you, something or someone who's blocking your way, keeping you from fully stepping into your power, all of the power you want and deserve?" Again, with the group nodding as if all of them were in a trance.

Wait? Some-*one*? *Someone*? This didn't seem right. But I'd already drawn too much attention to myself, become the butt of some joke that I didn't get. I'd stay in my place.

Luna continued, "We call upon our dark Father, Samiel, Lucifer Morningstar, the light-bearer! We are The Seven Sisters! Hear our pleas!"

"Hear our pleas!" The Six spoke in unison.

The fuck? What had I gotten myself into?

I had to get out of here, but the others had tight grips on my hands and my forearms, their fingers digging into my flesh.

Luna began to chant, "Oh dark Father, hear our pleas, take the one, the one who sees. She takes our power, dismissing our needs. Hear us, Father, we beg of you on bended knee."

Then, they all fell to the floor, pulling me down with them, the group genuflecting, all together, me in their grasp. They began to sway and convulse, all the while whispering, "Hear us, Father, Hear us, Father."

Luna, louder now, began anew, "Blood and bone, ash and death. Blood and bone, ash and death."

Fuck! My mind was swirling, the room spinning, tilting side to side. I was scared, really scared! And I couldn't get out, their hold on me, so tight! Their nails pierced my flesh, drawing blood now, my blood dripping into the circle.

All of them now, "Blood and bone, ash and death!" They repeated, over and over again. So loud, I couldn't think straight! "Blood and bone, Blood and bone!" Was I saying it now, too? The chant turned into moans; it was ecstatic, orgasmic even. It was some kind of magic I'd sure as shit never experienced myself! Writhing, limbs entwined, the energy rising, they all turned and twisted awkwardly on the floor. Their bodies gleaming with sweat. And I saw tails, ears, wings. Were they *transforming*? What the hell? Was I free? Had they let go? No, I was in it, down in the muck with them, swept away.

The movement, the music, (was there music?) the madness, the splendor, all of us caught up in a frenzy — then I heard a deep, throaty laugh, an unnatural sound, and my stupor was broken. There was something or someone there with us! And the smell. I smelled…eggs? Sulfur? Blood and bone, blood and bone. And then blackness…all light…gone. A scant bit of moonlight was all there was. I could see my breath. The attic had grown cold. Cold. What had they done? What had *I* done? Only one word came to my mind, and that was "Kelly."

CHAPTER 11

Kelly was dead.

I wasn't sure what had happened. But something felt...off. The morning after my experience with The Six, I'd called Mary in a panic. I kept trying to tell her something had happened, that something was very wrong. I didn't go into details. Finally, I convinced her to go with me to the hospital to check on Kelly.

They still weren't going to let us in. No family had shown up in all this time. I spied nursey-nurse over in the corner of the nurse's station, chewing on her cuticles. Mary was talking to the doctor assigned to Kelly. I made my way into a supply closet but cracked the door so I could hear. I don't know how she convinced him, but the doctor was offering more information than we'd gotten since Kelly's accident. Something about a long gap last night, the nurses *not* checking in on her regularly. Hmm, that's why nursey-nurse was off to the side, cowering. Kelly's blood...toxic...rapid onset of livor mortis...the hell? Never seen this before...

this setting in so quickly.

I took my chance then, while everyone was distracted, darted from the closet and snuck into Kelly's room. My God! My Goddess! I bit down on my lips to keep from screaming, pinching myself, hard, making myself look, see. She looked different, unrecognizable. She'd been bloodied and bruised before, but now, now, it's like the bruises had spread, like Kelly was one giant bruise. Her skin was completely discolored. I made myself edge closer to the bed, tears now streaming down my face. I lifted the blanket so I could see all of her. The stench, I turned away, trying to keep from throwing up. Rot. Death. She was purple and black from head to toe. There was no trace of the old Kelly. How, how could this have happened so fast? Why wasn't anyone checking in on her? Why, just why? But I knew. Deep down, I knew. And in that moment of realization, a part of me died, too, in that room with Kelly.

"Miss, Miss. You can't be here. You have to leave immediately!" It was that nurse *trying* to do her job. And she smelled like...like...cloves.

I went into the hall to find Mary and she

and the doctor just stopped their conversation and stared at me. I looked from Mary to the doctor and back to Mary. Then, I turned and ran down the hall and out of the hospital. I didn't stop until I got to my house.

~*~

The next week was a blur. T had tried to text me but I wasn't responding, ghosting her. My stepdad had heard about Kelly and had come over to check on me, making sure my prescriptions were filled and bringing me groceries and stuff. I appreciated it and promised I'd call if I needed him, but I really just wanted to be alone. I didn't *need* to be alone. I didn't do well left to my own devices, but I had a lot to think about. Not only about Kelly but about *that* night. I kept going over the night in my head during moments of lucidity — there weren't many of those because I kept myself well-medicated and washed it all down with wine. Red, red, wine. I took them all: "the one to relax," "the one to sleep," and "the one to perk me up" when I had to go to work or school.

Bennie had said I didn't have to come in, but it helped. I just tuned everything and everyone out, served customers, and went into robot mode. I kept going to school, too, but I wasn't running into T or The Six for some reason. And Ro. I'd been so stupid. She didn't like me. She had used me. The Six. They needed seven. Me and my blood. I was the seventh sister. And I knew. Whatever they had conjured up in the attic that night, whatever entity, it came from a dark place, a bad place. They had invoked a kind of magic I'd never experienced before. And I'd be lying if I said I wasn't intrigued, but...but...Kelly. I knew. It had all been about Kelly. She'd always given off this energy, this power, and I guess The Six had wanted it.

~*~

It had been over a month since Kelly had died. The so-called blood relations had finally come forward. They'd had her cremated, turned to ash, what with the condition of the body—an open casket was out of the question. *They* didn't want the funeral to be too close to Thanksgiving or Christmas so the service had been set for the first week of December. *They* had also made arrangements with a local church for the ceremony. That was *so* not Kelly. She'd have wanted it outside or anyplace else. I'm sure of it.

So here we were on the day of Kelly's funeral. I still couldn't believe this was really happening. I sat on the back row with the rest of the Woo Woo Girls, Mary and the crew, Bennie and Tristan, and the twins, Iris and Joyce—everybody was back in town now—and T. They were still my tribe, even though I'd defected on Halloween. Did they know? I mean, shit, there was no way they *could*, was there? They do have their ways, but no, there was no way they could know about the ritual I'd been a part of with The Six. Then, my thoughts drifted to Ro.

"I'm such a fucking idiot," I whispered under my breath.

"What?" T leaned over, thinking I was talking to her.

"Oh, nothing. Nothing." I covered it up and went back into my stupor. I sat there, all in black, which was my usual, flanked by all the gals in their black garb too. We must have looked like a coven, a coven I should have stayed with and not left, even if it was for just one night.

After the church stuff, there would be

something at the graveside too but it was particularly warm and sunny today, not a surprise for December in the south, and with my fair skin, I didn't want to fry. I'd only been outside for a few minutes and could already feel the sweat beginning to drip down the back of my neck. Outside of the church, the gals had gathered over to the side and were talking in hushed voices, looking right at me, wide-brimmed hats shading and hiding some of their faces. I could still feel their eyes, though. WTF. Did they know? I turned tail to make a quick exit when T caught up with me.

"Hey," T said and pulled me in for a hug. It had been a while since I'd had one of T's hugs. Since we'd been distant, I wasn't ready for it and stiffened under her embrace. The black silk flowers of her hat, Blossom-style, brushed my cheek. T was still T, styling, even at a funeral.

"Hey," was all I said back.

"I'm sorry I haven't been around much. I didn't know if you needed space or not to deal with all of this, and with Ro always around now…"

"Ro is *not* around!" I shot back. My softening was over. I had put my armor back on.

"Oh…I'm sorry for that, too. You, ok?"

"Fine. I'm fine."

We started to walk in silence, falling into step with one another, the way home embedded in our muscle memory. When we got to the crossroads, T stopped and let out a long exhale.

"I know this is awful timing, Elia, but I've got to tell you something. I've been putting it off, and I can't any longer.

I stood there, squinting in the midday sun, my hands pushing my hair behind my ears. "Well," I said, "What's up, T. Out with it."

"I'm, I'm leaving town. You remember that program abroad I applied to over the summer?"

I didn't but nodded yes anyway.

"Well, I got in! I know the timing could not be worse with Kelly's passing and all. I just wanted you to know."

"Fine. I mean, great, that's great news for you." My tone was not celebratory at all.

"And, Elia, I'm leaving…next week."

"The fuck, T. That's really soon!"

"I know, I know. My parents and I are leaving to spend the holidays there and they are going to help me settle in and all with the host family before the new year. I should have told you sooner. I just couldn't get a read on your mood these days, and of course, I was worried, what with your history and all."

My mood! My history! At this, I jutted my hip out, folded my arms, and drew my lips tightly together, a grim line slashing across my face.

"You know, T, it's *fine*. You go. I'm going to be *fine*. Don't you worry about me." The words spat from my lips like venom. I threw my arms in the air, flailing about, swatting at imaginary targets. Shit. I should take that back. I relaxed my body and took a deep breath, drawing the poison back into my own body. I tried to remember that this was my friend, my best friend. Then, more softly, I added, "No, T, really, it's all good, I am happy for you. You're going to do *great*."

I tried to initiate a hug then. It was hard. My body was not ready for contact with anyone. T didn't seem to mind. When I let her go, she held onto my hands and smiled at me. I tried to smile back, just barely lifting the corners of my lips.

"We should get together before I leave,

have a sleepover, watch some spooky movies, you know? Since we missed our annual Halloween ritual and all."

"Sure, T," I said, "Fine, that'll be fine." Huh. Did T know, too? There was no way she could know what really went down, no way in hell. Maybe she was just fishing, trying to see if I'd spill the tea.

T half-heartedly smiled at me and waved as she turned down the street to her house. As I watched her walk away, I knew we wouldn't be getting together before she left. I wondered if we'd ever get together again at all.

As I made my way down my own street, I felt the caress of those bony phantom fingers. Even if the Girls or T didn't know, the ghosts knew. They knew I'd crossed the line. They were waiting for me to drown myself in my misery, me all too vulnerable, and them wanting to pull me over to the other side to join The Horrifying Women.

CHAPTER 12

I woke up late the next day, sunlight blaring through my window. I was still in my clothes from Kelly's funeral. I spied an empty bottle on the floor. I glanced over at my desk—medication bottles knocked over. I felt like I'd been hit in the back of the head with a 2x4. I tried to remember what had happened last night when I got home. Thinking only of myself and my misery, I'd forgotten to leave the rosemary and the glass of spirits for the spirits in the bathroom. Yeah, just myself and my misery. I'd thrown a little pity party last night. Late last night, I'd been lulled to sleep, drifting off in a sea of wine and pills and thoughts of Ro.

I let myself get taken in by Ro. She had set out the bait, and I'd taken it, letting my hormones take over. Fuck. Now, in the light of day, I tried to go back and think about it all, remembering what had happened in Luna's attic that night. I know one thing; we called in some kind of force using directed or combined energy—I read about this shit before. We'd all manifested it. Shit, they'd needed me to pull it off, and I was lonely, horny, curious. They had wanted to gain some kind of power, and I guess they thought Kelly had power they could usurp. And they needed ME. I made Seven. I'd joined in right along with them. And we, I don't know, invited something or someone in. I remember sensing something taking up the space, smelling something putrid, and hearing something…evil. I pulled my knees into my chest, trying to make myself small, like a child scared to let their feet dangle off the side of the mattress, not knowing if something or someone might snatch them from underneath the bed.

I stayed that way for a long time.

THEN

I'd had nightmares a lot when I was a kid. Or maybe they were stress dreams. There were the reoccurring drowning kind, where I was stuck in a pool or lake, my suit caught on something, the water rising, and I couldn't get out. Then, there were the stair ones. There were several old buildings in town, one being the church Mom dragged me to a few times, with that old late 60s/

early 70s design with floating staircases. These scared the shit out of me! In these dreams, I'd be at the top of the stairs, the steps too far down, too far apart, too narrow. I couldn't move. I was frozen in place, paralyzed by the fear of falling.

I can't remember exactly when the bad dreams started, but I had a pretty good idea when they got worse. In the 5th grade, my teacher was reading *The Amityville Horror* and regaling us all with a play-by-play of whatever chapter she was currently on. Yeah, great idea to share this with a bunch of 10- and 11-year-olds. That was when I'd wanted to ditch my box springs and bedframe and sleep on a mattress on the floor. That way, the monsters couldn't hide.

Nightmares have gotten worse over the years. I remember once dreaming about the devil and possession (maybe I'd snuck in a viewing of *The Exorcist* late one night). In this dream, I was running and running through the house, trying to get to Mom's room, trying to get help. It was like that old scene from *Poltergeist* that T and I had watched. Jo Beth Williams running and running down the hall trying to rescue her little girl from the monsters. I never made it, neither in my dream state nor my waking life, for that matter. Nobody was ever going to save me. Awake or asleep, I had to live with the monsters.

NOW

Days passed. I'd managed to make it to enough classes to finish up the semester, barely passing my exams. I had begun to spread out my therapy appointments, showing up often enough to get my prescriptions. I'd stopped going to work. Bennie and Tristan had texted at first, then called and called, leaving voicemails, but I didn't respond. Finally, after about two weeks, my stepdad came over to the house.

He found me lying on the couch in the dark. He opened a set of blinds. I groaned and turned my head into the cushions.

"Hey, kiddo," he said, jostling me a little, "You gonna sleep all day?"

"Hey," I managed, pushing myself upright, "What time is it anyway?" Fuck. I didn't even know what day it was. My stepdad sat next to me, staring straight ahead, looking out the window.

"Elia, I have to say, you've looked better, heh, heh. But I know teenagers, late to bed, late to get up, eh? You having fun on your break?"

On my break? Oh. I remember finishing exams. It must be getting close to the holidays. "Yeah, something like that. You know, watching movies, hanging with friends..."

"Elia, I checked out the kitchen before I woke you up. There's hardly any food in there at all. You could have called. You know you always can, kiddo. You can always call...and Elia, I know about T being abroad and, and I know about Kelly too. I'm really sorry."

I put my head in my hands, rubbing my forehead. "Thanks," was all I could utter at this point, still trying to wake up.

My stepdad looked down now, hands clasped in his lap. "Kiddo, I have to tell you something. It's not easy. Look, I've gotten a job offer out of state, and, and, I'm taking it." Still not looking at me, he went on, "Elia, I want you to know I'm not just abandoning you and your mother."

Mother. Geez. I'd put her somewhere else in

my head, forgetting she even existed.

"I still want to help out financially, and, and..." He was walking over to the window now. "Looky here, kid," he said, gesturing to the driveway.

I got up to see what he was pointing at. A car. A car! I couldn't freaking believe it! I gave him a huge hug, and he backed up a bit, pulling me in for a quick side hug. Neither of us were the touchy-feely kind.

"Thank you, thank you so much! I don't know what to say." Then, I remembered he'd said he was moving. Wait. What?

"Think of it as an early Christmas gift, Elia. Now, like I said, I'm going to be moving. Well, most of my things have been shipped already. But...I'll still send you money and help you out with the car and health insurance. You've got a semester left of high school and I want you to see it through, get off to college even. And as far as food..." He paused, his eyes lingering over the trash on the coffee table, half empty mugs, cans, chip bags, microwave meals, the food remains in the dishes, dark and crusted over. "We'll go today.

I'm going to take you to Snack and Pack and set up an account for you. You can get food, whatever you need there. Perhaps garbage bags, disinfectant?"

That was one thing about small, southern towns. You could still run a tab at some places, get billed, and pay at the end of the month. The market was next door to Franks' Pizza and Ice Cream Shack and I was hoping I could extend my bill over there as well. I couldn't believe this was happening! I'd *really* be all on my own. All. On. My. Own. T was gone, albeit temporarily. My stepdad was leaving. I was probably fired from *BB's*, and fuck if I'd have anything to do with Ro or The Five, er, Six anymore. And, Kelly...but...I could get whatever I wanted, huh? I was wondering if booze fell under that category.

"Okay, kiddo. I said I'd take you, but now YOU can take me. Let's try out the new car, go for a spin, huh?" He said, dangling the keys in my face.

"Sure. That sounds great!" I said, feeling better than I had in a long time.

"And, Elia, you'll need to check your voicemail more regularly. You'll be Mom's contact since you're the closest relative. The Spa may need to reach you. Oh, and kiddo, why don't you jump in the shower first? You could use one."

~*~

Christmas had come and gone along with New Year's Eve. I'd put on something semi-clean that day my stepdad came over, but now I was resigned to the vintage dress I'd found in the attic. I was in mourning, after all. I'd gotten a good haul on the grocery run with my stepdad, food, toilet paper, shit like that, oh, and more red wine. Just a few days ago, I'd driven back to the market, gotten some crackers and chips, and picked up the refills on my meds. And just like I'd suspected, they let me put more wine on my tab. They say the drinking age in the South is whenever you're tall enough to reach the bar, so...

I was hanging out in my room mostly, watching movies, streaming. I was totally disconnected, emotionally and spiritually. I was zoned out. The only thing I was managing to do well was keep myself doped up. No homework over break and I'd put that self-portrait project in the back of my mind. I wasn't even doing the nightly ritual anymore. It didn't seem to matter anyway. I hadn't noticed anything strange. Just this weird odor, but after what my stepdad had said the last time he was here, I figured it was just me and my lack of hygiene. I looked at my phone for the first time in a while. The last text I'd gotten was from Tristan telling me not to bother to come into the coffee shop anymore. I guess I'd been fired. Bennie would have sugar-coated it, but Tristan just shot from the hip. I had some notifications in my voicemail. It might be The Spa since I was now the closest contact person. That news alone made me want to retch, so I chose to ignore the growing numbers in the little red square. When I put down my phone, it fell to the floor. I leaned over the side of my bed, reaching for it, and noticed that shoe box I'd never looked in since bringing it down from the attic.

The box was full of old pictures. I sat in the middle of my bed, looking through family photos. The box must have been Mother's or maybe my Aunt Laera's. In the first pic, I recognized my grandmother standing at the kitchen sink. I saw her eyes, Mom's eyes, my eyes — all of us sharing this feature — her head craned towards the camera, a cigarette dangling from her lips. There was my mom, maybe 7 or 8, sitting on the floor underfoot, and my Aunt Laera, probably around 17 years old, leaning against the fridge, all of them in the kitchen at my grandmother's house, no one smiling. My Aunt was beautiful! She, like my mother, had the same eyes and hair, only a lighter shade of blonde, more like mine, really.

Sifting through the stack, I found more of the same. Pictures of the three of them. No one smiling in any photo. And then, I came across one of my Aunt by herself. She was standing outside in a park, maybe. She looked like she had paused mid-spin, her dress, the very dress I was wearing, flaring out around her, a smile as brilliant as the sun shining down on her, illuminating her. Her arms reaching for the sky. Wait. On the inside of her wrist, I saw it. That tattoo, the symbol for The Order of Lilith. Could it be? Had my Aunt been a Woo Woo Girl or...I...I couldn't even say it out loud...a...a... witch? I jumped up, stumbling a bit, my head spinning. It could have been the aftereffects of my med/wine dinner from the night before, though. I shook my head to clear out the cobwebs and took a deep breath. Steadying myself, I ran down to the kitchen to get the key from the junk drawer and then up to the attic to see what else was in that old trunk.

Brrr. Yeah, It was January, but I lived in the south. It wouldn't be *that* cold *inside*. Through Mom's old, empty room and into the smaller attic space. It was still daylight. Some light was creeping in through that high window. I could see well enough to get around. I sat crisscrossed on the dusty floor and opened the trunk.

I rifled through a few more pieces of old clothes, nothing exciting. I pushed them aside along with the other shoe box I'd left the last time I was rooting around in there, hoping to find out more about my Aunt Laera, but at the bottom of the trunk, what, a game box? The front was faded, and I couldn't quite make out what it was. I put the box down and ran my hand over the lid. Parcheesi? I opened it, and well, well, well. Another old game lay nestled inside, Parker Brothers, circa 1970. There was nothing else in the box. No instructions or anything. I took the game and locked up behind myself. Why? There was no one ever here but me.

Back in my room, I sat down on my bed with the board, tracing over the letters, the numbers, the moon, the sun. I knew nothing about how to use one of these things, but I did know that you needed another piece? I decided to consult my modern-day grimoire. Google search: "How do you use an Ouija board?"

~*~

I gathered the things I needed to use the Ouija board or what I thought I should use. The instructions or rules I found online were few, but I did remember that I'd read that it was important to say "GOODBYE" at the end of the session, oh, and to "NEVER USE IT ALONE." I kept finding *that* tidbit in all caps. Well, fuck, I *was* alone, so I'd just count that as three: me, myself, and I.

I had the board. I grabbed a lighter and my sage. I knew enough to smudge the space. I was about to pour two glasses of wine and thought, what the hell, and just opened a new bottle and put the glasses back in the cabinet. Now, I'd have to get creative. I didn't have that planchette thingy, so what could I use? There was an old iron trivet shaped like a spade near the stovetop. It would have to do.

Heading back up the stairs, I thought, *Oh shit! I forgot my meds today, whatever day it was.* I stopped in my room and again thought, what the hell? I'd just take the "something for relaxation" *and* "something to pep me up." Seemed like they'd be at odds with each other, but...I wasn't feeling like myself these days, and I needed all the help I could get. Popping them into my mouth along with a couple of pain relievers, I washed them down with a couple of swigs of red.

Back in the attic, I smudged a little and drank a little. Rinse, repeat. I sat in the center of the attic space with the board in front of me. The sun had gone down by now, and I had to use my phone for light. It was dark, but I could still see a little. Hmm. I hadn't thought what I'd do or who I'd try to contact. Maybe Aunt Laera? Maybe it was finally time I figured out why she was sticking around. I breathed deeply and placed my hands on the trivet.

I moved the trivet in counterclockwise circles to warm up the board. Then, I stopped and focused my energy. Closing my eyes, I took in another deep breath and asked, "Is there anyone here?" The trivet trembled all on its own. It quickly slid over to YES. Ok! This may work! I could feel something, sense something behind me. "Aunt Laera?" I said aloud, quietly, not sure if I really wanted to communicate with the spirits. Nothing. I spoke again, louder this time, "Aunt Laera, are you here?" I smelled vanilla, like the smell of a doughnut shop when the fresh ones were still hot. Then, I felt a hand touching my hair gently. I froze, afraid to turn around.

I sat up tall, shoulders back, pressing my lips together, and turned to look over my shoulder. Slowly, I opened my eyes, and there she was! Only this time, she was not the mass of loose skin and greasy hair I'd seen that first time in my bathroom. She looked exactly like the photo I'd found. She was beautiful, hovering behind me, with light blond hair, and her eyes, my eyes, gazed at me for only a second, and she was gone. And the smell of pastries along with her. And, and, now, another smell was present. Eggs, definitely rotten eggs.

Turning back to the board, frightened but staying the course. Placing my now shaking hands on the trivet, I asked again, "Is anyone *else* here?"

YES YES YES YES YES YES YES YES YES YES YES YES YES YES!!!!!!!!!!!

Over and over, my hands were pulled to the corner to the word YES, the trivet now boring tracks into the game board.

Besides feeling scared shitless, I started to feel woozy. But doing what I could to gather my senses, I asked another question, "Who is here?"

The trivet began to vibrate with energy. It jumped from letter to letter. First A. Then, S. Then, M. Then...This was *not* Aunt Laera! The smell, malodorous and stronger now, causing me to retch, my stomach heaving and lurching. Before any more letters were made clear, I saw her! Aunt Laera floating in the corner of the attic. She gestured to the board, sending the trivet flying through the air. I sat there for a moment in a state of wonder and disbelief.

Aunt Laera was staring at something or someone. I looked around the room, but I couldn't make anything out! I sensed...a presence. Then, out of nowhere, I heard that deep, throaty laugh, the one I'd heard at Luna's house on Samhain. Aunt

Laera looked at me now. My dry heaves turned into vomit, and I spewed red wine and bile across the room. The vomiting ceased momentarily, long enough for a low wail and a deafening scream to emerge from *my* throat! I felt like my heart and my soul were being twisted and torn from my body. I fell over forward. Something or someone was taking over. Lifting my head from a pool of slime, the last thing I saw was Aunt Laera, tears streaming down her face.

I tried as hard as I could to go to her, reach her, but she disappeared into thin air. I puked again. I didn't know what the fuck was happening to me. My body began to contort, my arms flailing. I began to claw at my arms and legs like I was desperately trying to get out of my skin. And then, as though lightning shot through my spine, I flew up into the air, hitting the ceiling. And then, down I went, collapsing onto the floor. But I remembered. Only one more sound escaped my lips, "GOODBYE."

~*~

Where was I? I didn't know what time it was or even what day it was. As my eyes adjusted to the light, faces began to take shape. All of the Girls were here, and it looked like The Phantom Finders were here too. I sat up and looked around the room. My head was spinning. Bennie was here, and Tristan was sitting on the floor in the corner.

"Elia, you're back with us!" Mary said, coming over and pushing my hair out of my face.

"How...when...what?" I was babbling, struggling to string words together.

Bennie spoke up now, "Well, when you stopped showing up for work, Tristan decided to go over to your house and see what was up."

I looked back over at Tristan. She was biting her thumbnail, looking at me sideways, and shrugging one shoulder.

"Where am I?"

Bennie continued. "Well, hon, you're at my little apartment around the corner from BB's. As I said, Tristan found you, called all of us, and we showed up at your house. Tristan and I got you cleaned up and brought you here while Mary and the others straightened things up in your attic. Elia, do you remember anything at all?"

Before I could utter a word, Mary cut in. "It

was quite the disaster area, Elia," and the others nodded along in unison. "And, Elia, we took that old Ouija board." I must have looked surprised or hurt, and Mary quickly added, "Now, we still have it, but the sisters have been working on it, clearing the negative energy. Wiping the slate, as it were."

With the mention of the Ouija board, bits and pieces began to come back. I remembered being in the attic. I remembered trying to make contact with Aunt Laera? But...but...I cried out, my hand covering my outburst, my eyes wide. I remembered a feeling, a presence, something awful, but I couldn't think straight, the memories all fuzzy around the edges.

Bennie and Mary came over now and sat on either side of the bed, trying to comfort me. And it was then that I saw *her*. Ro. She was lurking in the door jamb. My fear and sadness quickly turned to anger.

"What the hell is *she* doing here?" I blurted out, about to lunge at her from across the room.

"Now, Elia. Ro is here to help." It was Tristan, standing now, coming to Ro's defense.

"But...but...but..." I was so furious it was

all I could get out.

Tristan started again, "Elia, Ro told us everything about The Six, about Samhain, about her part...in it all."

I was mortified. Now, they *all* knew. I was fucking humiliated. It was all so embarrassing.

"Elia, I'm sorry, I, I..." Ro was attempting to, what, apologize?

I couldn't even look at her. "Save it, Ro," I said, "I'm not ready to make nice." And with that, she crept back towards the hall, but she didn't leave.

Mary, ever the fearless leader, took over now, motioning for Tristan to sit back down. "Elia, Ro did tell us everything. It was big of her. She really is concerned about you. I can only imagine what you're feeling right now. I know you're hurt. You feel betrayed, and you have every right to feel that way. But we can address those wounds later. Now, I want to talk about the night of Samhain and how you ended up in a puddle of vomit in your attic."

I looked down, wringing my hands in my lap. Ugh. A puddle of puke. Just another graphic picture of the mess I'd made of things. Lovely.

"Ro told us about the ritual that Luna involved you in. She told us about how she flirted with you, lured you, for lack of a better word, and delivered you to the others that night. Ro also told us about taking the bloody tissue from your house and using it in a different spell that The Six performed to ensure that you'd join them that night, also, about you bringing your own blood to their gathering. Elia, I'm not here to chastise you, but you know better about blood rituals. I know you do."

Chastise *me*? She'd basically just said the Ro had groomed me. I let out a sigh and rolled my eyes to the ceiling now. Shit, I knew it. And shit, I knew it wasn't all Ro. I was a willing participant. I did not want to acknowledge it, but it was true.

Bennie was up now, "Elia, like Mary said, we cleaned everything up, and the twins are working on the board, but that's not everything that needs to be done. I think, I mean, I feel fairly sure, hon, that you called something into your house. We'll have to do a proper clearing and a blessing. It's almost time for school to start back up. T will be coming back into town soon. We'll all work together; we'll help you set things right at home. And Elia, we want to help you get back on track. All of this, plus Kelly's passing—it's been a lot. It would be a lot for anyone. But you know," she said now, cradling my chin in her hands, "You know, hon, with your history, well, some of us just have to work a little bit harder at life than others. Later, when you feel up to it, we're going to tidy up the rest of your house, make sure you have everything you need, and you know, you'll need to get back with your counselor, and then maybe, you'll be ready to come back to work too. But there's no rush, hon."

Mary and the Girls must have filled in the rest of them with my *history*. Again, I was humiliated. I wished the ground would just swallow me up. But I knew Bennie was right. I had to get my shit together. I wanted to finish high school. I could trust them, well, not *all* of them. I still wasn't ready to see or talk to Ro. Fuck her and The Six, for that matter. It would take some serious groveling on her part to move me at all. And T. I missed her. I needed to see her.

It would take time and work, but I could do

it again. I'd let the wine and the meds take over. I'd been living in a stupor and wallowing in self-pity. If I stayed in this state, I'd throw away all of the hard work I'd done over the years. I'd be giving into my DNA right along with The Horrifying Women in my family. And Kelly. She'd be disappointed. Knowing that was enough to get me motivated, up and moving. I tried to stand, but the room went all catawampus. When *had* I eaten last? My stomach felt empty. I was starving. A burger. Protein. I needed meat. A nice, red, bloody burger.

CHAPTER 13

It was February. Winter in the south. One week, it would be humid in the high seventies, with people running around in shorts. The next, it would drop to the low 30s, and all of the summer-lovers would be grumbling in their North Face fleece and Uggs. Mardi Gras parades rolled through town, children ran and played in the middle of the road, and the streets closed off. It was loud and bright, and most folks were in high celebration mode. I would just throw on my old navy pea coat and muddle through. I myself was *not* in the carnival spirit. But I loved those cold, cloudy days. It was the perfect time to walk by the bay and watch the water. I needed to think.

After waking up that time at Bennie's, I'd just been taking life one day at a time. The Girls had bailed me out, all of them, including Bennie AND Tristan, of all people. Even though it seemed quiet at my house, no unexplained visits from the beyond, The Spector Specialists showed up to perform a ritual. They asked to be alone in the attic but I peeked in through the keyhole to see what they were up to. Still, I had no clue what they were doing. All they did was stand on opposite sides of the room, make weird gestures with their index fingers, and whisper under their breath. They still hadn't returned my Ouija board.

After all of that, the Girls left town. It was sad and strange not to have them around but after the hurricane last fall, they had decided to move permanently. Getting up there in years, most of them wanted to be closer to family. Something I couldn't relate to, wanting to be near family. I'd started back into regular therapy almost immediately. Then, T came back from her study abroad program. It turned out that it was only a 4-week course study. I had her come over to my house so I could surprise her with the news of my new car. Give her the good news before filling her in on everything else that had happened.

I'd gone back to work at *BB's* on a very part-time basis. I was still recovering from everything that had gone down. Tristan seemed nicer. She wasn't as curt with me these days and I hadn't given much thought as to what had brought this change about. But I did notice that she had gotten new ink. She now had the same tat on her right shoulder that Bennie had on her neck and that Kelly had on her wrist. One day, I'd like to ask her about The Order of Lilith.

The Satanic Six weren't loitering around the storefront anymore. No more stepping over them through a cloud of clove-scented smoke to get in the door. I'd heard through the grapevine that they'd opted for virtual school. All of them but Ro. I still see her at school, trying to make eye contact with me, but I did my best to avoid her.

Everything in the shop was decked out for Valentine's Day. It made me want to gag. I was practicing making hearts in a latte when T came in for coffee. She was in head-to-toe pink. She didn't make me want to gag, though. That was T, dressing for the season. And it was one of her best colors.

"Hey, bestie. This one's for you," I said as I gently pushed the drink towards her, my wanky foam heart floating around in a froth at the top of the mug.

"Thanks, Elia," she said, taking the cup in one hand. Then she placed her other hand over mine and whispered, "How are you doing? You, okay?"

I recoiled slightly from her. *Everyone*, it seemed, was worried about me, and I really did *not* like being the center of attention in this way. If I wasn't getting the "Are you okay?" question, I was getting the soft-tight-smile-furrowed-forehead look which suggested the same. T felt it. I knew it because then she gave me the pinched brows.

"Ah, sorry, T. I'm fine. Good. Everything's fine." I even attempted a smile.

"That's good to hear. I was hoping things were getting better. Can you believe it's already February? I can't! We really only have about three more months of school, then finals, then graduation!" T sipped her latte, licking away her foam mustache.

"Yep," I said, wiping the counter, "That's right."

"And you know what else? Prom!!! It's going to be so much fun! Then…our last sweet summer by the bay…before college," she said wistfully, her voice dropping to a hush with that last sentence.

It was my turn to reach out. "I know," I

said, patting her hand. "I know. Hey, let's do something this weekend. You wanna come over, get pizzas, watch movies? My treat. We'll just charge everything to the Step."

T was back to T in an instant, her face brightening. "Yes, yes, yes! What are you in the mood for?"

"Oh, I don't know. How about something classic…like *The Exorcist* with Linda Blair?"

T's forehead wrinkled again at this. "Are you sure? I mean, after all the shit that went down over break? Do we, do *you* need to watch something so unnerving?"

"Yeah, sure. Saturday night. Let's do it."

T just nodded yes slowly, turning to leave *BB's* with her coffee. Usually, I went in for monsters, vamps, and classic slashers. I don't know why, but *The Exorcist* had just popped into my head. Just a feeling.

T showed up Saturday night for our girl's night in. She was wearing a plain red t-shirt and black fleece jammie bottoms covered in bright fuchsia hearts. Oh shit! Was *today* Valentine's Day? It had totally slipped my mind. I really was a shit friend.

T looked at me, standing there in my usual mourning garb, reached into her tote and pulled out a large heart-shaped box of candy from the drugstore, and handed it to me with a huge toothy smile. It was a sweet gesture, but yeah, I sure as shit had forgotten what today was.

"Oh, T. This, this is so nice. I..." I said moving my hand up and down, weighing the chocolates.

"Elia, it's ok, really. No biggie."

But I could tell she was hurt. She'd never, ever show it, though.

"My folks got me candy and a plushie. I'm good, really. I just figured..."

Just figured...I'd be alone, forgotten. My imaginary relationship with Ro over and done with. My stepdad, wherever the hell he was.

"Thanks, T. For thinking of me."

T gave me the hug I always needed. Everything was right with the world again.

"C'mon," I said, jangling my keys. "Let's bolt."

Taking off in *my* car, we headed for Frank's where we got a heart-shaped pie, half cheese and mushroom, half meat lovers. T never asked me about my sudden shift from vegetarianism. She just always rolled with whatever crap I threw out there. Then, we went next door to the Snack and Pack and picked up diet soda and wine. T gave me a sideways glance when I grabbed a bottle of red but didn't say a word about it. And no one in the store batted an eye since I had an account. We were all set.

Back at my house, we took everything up to my room and set up my laptop, ready for a night of thrills and chills. Eating pizza right out of the box, we sat there, glued to the screen, watching Linda Blair's transformation from a seemingly normal kid to a demon possessed freak! About the time Regan started spewing split pea soup, T shut the top of my computer.

"That's it, Elia! That is all I can take."

"Aw, c'mon, T. Don't cha want to see what happens?"

"No. No. And NO! Elia, that movie is scaring the crap out of me! How am I going to sleep tonight or ever again?"

"Huh, I think it's kind of interesting."

"Interesting? That is the *last* word I would use to describe *The Exorcist*, Elia."

"Ok, Ok, I get it. I'll watch the rest later, alone," I said, wiggling woo woo fingers in T's face.

"Well, that'll be much later. Right now, I have got to watch something else, something light, a rom com or something, anything. I need the eye bleach. But first, I need to pee."

"No, no T! Me first. I've had to go so bad ever since that peeing on the floor scene."

"Ew. Fine. I can wait. But leave the door open in case I get scared and need to holler at you."

"Sure, T."

In the hall bath, I left the door ajar and hurriedly squatted on the toilet and let out the piss I'd been holding in. After what seemed like forever, I got up and went to the sink to wash my hands. The water was running clear. At first. Then, after a couple of sputters, it turned black and thick. Oh shit. Oh shit. Nothing had happened in a while. What the fuck? And then, the long, gray hairs. Strands and strands of slimy, stringy hair were running out of the faucet, filling the sink.

I must have screamed because T came running in. I didn't want to freak her out, so I moved in front of the sink, trying to shield her from what was happening.

"It's, it's, it's ok, T. Nothing. It's nothing. Really, it's nothing."

She pushed past me and turned off the water. I covered my face with my hands.

"Elia, what on earth were you screaming about?"

"You, You don't *see* it?"

"I don't see anything, Elia. What's going on?"

I moved my fingers apart, peeking through the gaps. Nothing. There was nothing in the sink.

"Oh, well, shit, T. Maybe that flick scared me more than I thought. I could have sworn..." Again, I didn't want T to wig out. "Nothing. My imagination is just running in overdrive."

"Ok, then. I'm going to pee next and let's find something funny or an oldie, like *Breakfast at Tiffany's*. What do you think?"

I just nodded, and we headed back to my room, bleaching our eyes as T had said. But I couldn't concentrate on anything. Why couldn't T see what I saw? What if, what if, I'd never seen anything in the house? What if I was losing my mind? 'They're coming to take me away, ha, ha.' Maybe *I* belonged at The Spa. Maybe I was just as nuts as the rest of them, The Horrifying Women.

After the movie, I walked T to the door. She was back to herself, Audrey Hepburn, and George Peppard, her panacea. She hugged me bye and headed home.

I decided to pour myself some wine. Hell, I took the bottle up to my room, washed down my meds, and thought I'd try to finish *The Exorcist*. But before I got too comfy, I looked at my phone — it was at 17%. I noticed I had a number of missed calls, all from the same number. I knew what this was. I sat there, listening to my voicemails. So. Many. Voicemails. They'd been trying to reach me. They said Mother was not doing well. I needed to go to The Spa as soon as I could. They said, "Come…before it's too late." I barely made it to the bathroom before I started puking, projectile vomiting just like Regan. We were two green peas in a pod.

~*~

The next day, I tried to psyche myself up for a visit with Mom. My head was killing me, the combination of wine and pills, and I was still trying to figure out if I was really seeing things happen in the house after last night in the bathroom. I took my "something to pep me up," painted my lips, made myself a go cup of black coffee, got into my car, and headed to The Spa.

In the silence, my mind drifted from the fucked-up happenings in my home to my found family — all of the girls — T, Mary, and the Gals, Iris, Joyce, Bennie, Tristan, Ro. Did Ro belong in my circle? There was no fucking way I was ready to forgive her. But…if I'd learned anything from my 18 years on earth plus loads of therapy, I'd knew about forgiving. From T. T, always, always forgave me for messing up. And quick. I had to admit there were good women in my life. Maybe I could do it. Maybe Ro was different than the others. I had to put that thought away for now. I'd pulled up to The Spa, and it was time to see the not so good woman.

It had been months since I'd been here. I

walked onto the property, taking in the bare trees and the gray, weathered exterior of the institution. When I walked through the entrance, the smell of ammonia and urine hit me in the face, and I had to breathe through my mouth. I went through the motions, signing in at the guest check-in, opening my bag so this nursey-nurse could have a quick look-see, checking for weapons, perhaps. I mentioned that Mother had been moved, and I wasn't sure where her new room was.

My feet took me to the stairs and I made my way down to the 'special' area, the last stop. As I stood outside of her door, afraid to look into the small, square window, I remembered my last visit. It all came back like a living nightmare.

THEN

The fight, not the first between a mother and a daughter. Still wondered if it was a battle or a war. We'd tussled about, and Mom discovered my injury, my handiwork. She couldn't play second fiddle, and I watched. I watched her come completely undone. Wielding her homemade prison weapon, her shiv, she sliced into herself and began to feast on her own flesh! It was sickening. So. Much. Blood. That's when I knew she'd gone over the edge. She wasn't coming at me anymore. I felt pity as I finally looked away from the terror, sounding the alarm, calling the men in the white coats.

NOW

It seemed like that had happened so long ago, but it was only last summer, and I'd packed that memory away, refusing to look at it. Placing my hand on the door handle, I took one last, long, deep breath and went into her room.

The blinds were closed. It was dark, the only light coming from the machines keeping her alive. Was she *that* far gone? I couldn't help but feel a little relief. Would it finally all be over? I wish I could say I'd done the work to sever the ancestral ties, but maybe death was the only way. My eyes adjusted, and I could make out her form under the bedcovers. Her eyes were closed, tubes were coming out of her nose and arms. I walked over to her side and just stared. She looked so helpless. Her hands were on her stomach, one laying on top of the other. I reached out and gently held the top one in mine. Her eyes flew open, and she slowly turned her head towards me. Then, her eyes narrowed, and a tight grin spread across her chapped lips.

I didn't know what to do. I placed her hand back on her stomach and stepped back from the bed. Damnit! I tried not to show it, but she still scared the shit out of me. She let out this low, guttural chuckle, which turned into a wheezing cough. When she was able to quiet herself, I could hear the soft beeps sounding from her monitors. Then, she motioned to me with one long, crooked finger.

"Come closer, Elia," her voice raspy. "Come."

In my head, I knew she was too weak to do anything to me, but still...I didn't move.

"Elia," Mom was barely audible now.

I concentrated on the beeps, the rhythm like a drum, calling me as I moved towards her.

She crooked her finger again, indicating I should move closer. Her eyes, my eyes, met my gaze for a second as I moved past her head and put my ear near her mouth. The better to hear.

"Elia. Elia, my God, you stink." Still her surly self, verbal warfare.

"Elia."

I leaned closer, her fetid breath on my skin.

"Elia. Elia. I'm...not...your...mother."

The pattern of beeps ended abruptly, only one sustained sound remained, the pitch offensive, final. I looked at the screen, and one continual flat line etched its way across. That was it. Mother was gone.

CHAPTER 14

Holy shit! Did what just happen, *happen*? I left Mother's room in a daze. She was really gone. Ding dong, the witch was dead. I couldn't help but smile a little, swallowing my relief, my glee. I had to hide my feelings, meeting with the staff, going through the motions, and planning for her cremation. I tried to call my stepdad, straight to voicemail. We'd have to connect eventually, deciding where Mom's ashes would go. It would take over a week to get them back.

Driving back, my brain fog began to clear. Then, I remembered...

"Elia."

"Elia."

"I'm...not...your...mother."

I slammed on my brakes, causing the car behind me to almost rear-end me, the driver racing by, cutting in front of me, and flipping me off as they sat on their horn. Pulling over on the shoulder, I turned off the engine.

"I'm not your mother."

The words, her last words, played over and over again in my mind. On the one hand, I felt relief. Mom was not my mom. On the other hand, who the hell was my mom? What the hell had happened? I just sat there, alone in my car in the quiet, the occasional sound of another car heading down the road. I had to find answers. Maybe there were clues somewhere. I'd been through the trunk in the attic, but there was still that box marked BOOKS. Maybe there was something in there. Finally, I turned the key in the ignition and started for home.

I stopped off for another pizza, Italian sausage and bacon, from Frank's and picked up a couple of bottles of wine at The Snack and Pack. Then, I texted T, asking her to come over. That was all. I'm sure she just thought I was setting up a regular scare fest movie night in; I sure as shit couldn't tell her this kind of news in a text. I needed to tell her everything in person.

T was sitting on my bed. We were eating pizza, straight out of the box. T with her water flask. Me, drinking red straight from the bottle. T didn't even blink at this. Then, I spilled the tea, only it wasn't like a couple of old Southern broads gossiping. This info, well, it was its own kind of scare fest. A waking nightmare, really.

I stopped talking and looked at my bestie. Insert crickets chirping. T just sat there, her mouth hanging open mid-bite. She'd dropped everything, her pizza making a grease stain on my comforter, her water bottle now rolling along my bedroom floor. And then, she had her own what-the-fuck moment.

"WTF, Elia. Oh. My. God. Are you ok? I mean, my God. How? What?"

"How, what? What part, T?"

"Well, all of it, I guess. So…your Mom… or 'not your mom'…is…dead. Elia, I'm so *sorry*? I don't know what to say…just, my God, Elia."

"I know. It's this. It's all like an A24 WTF moment. Only it's not a horror movie. It's my life."

T reached out then, putting one hand over mine, comforting me. "Well, what's next?"

"I need to get in touch with my stepdad, or is he still my stepdad? I don't even know anymore. I've got to figure out what to do with Mom's or 'not my mom's' remains. And then, I've got to try to find out who my mother *is*."

"Right. And I'll help you however I can. First, I'll help you clean up the house some and then we need to talk seriously about your current coping tools. I've kept quiet, let you do what you need to do to get through, but the wine, your meds..." She cut her eyes over to the pharmacy on my desktop. "It's too much, Elia. We're almost done with school. You can't start college this way. You're my friend, and I want to help, k? This haze you're living in, day to day, you're not really living. You're in a fog. It's not healthy."

I bristled at this. I did not want to hear it. I didn't want to let go. I was holding on tight to my stuff. But I knew she was right. Fuck. It would mean more therapy, maybe even a substance support group. I shuddered, cringing at this thought. I did, I wanted to go to college, and T was right. I couldn't get anywhere like this. Plus, once I started digging and trying to figure out all of my family stuff, I'd definitely need more counseling. I didn't say anything. I just nodded in agreement and let her hug me.

Walking T to the door, she leaned in for one

more hug. "Ok, bestie. Tomorrow, we start new. Or you start new, and I'm here for it all. Just let me know what the plan is and I'm on board, k?"

"Yeah, for sure. I'll shoot you a text after I make a few calls tomorrow."

"Great! Then, we can start talking about school, too. We really only have less than half of a semester left! Then prom, graduation…and…"

T's voice dropped out. I knew she was thinking about college. She'd be moving away, and I, more than likely, would be going somewhere local.

"And…and," That was all she got out before she pulled me in for a really tight hug, choking on her tears. Pulling away, she wiped her eyes and looked at me, "Check in with me later, k?"

"Sure. I will. You know, it's not all bad. I am finally…free." And with this, I grinned a little maniacally, giving T the crazy eyes.

"Well, yes, there's that." She paused, lingering in the porch light, and then, "Oh, one last thing, Elia. I know it's almost March, and it's not technically ever winter in our town but you ever think about running the heat in here, maybe? It's fricking freezing in your house!"

Huh, I hadn't noticed. Maybe I was used to it. Walking inside, I passed the kitchen, turning off the downstairs lights as I went. Before going into my room, I went up to Mom's/not my mom's room. I stood on the threshold, looking around. Exhaling, I could see my breath forming a small cloud in front of my face. Maybe T was right. Maybe it was too cold. But I didn't *feel* cold. As I turned to leave, I heard something. But it wasn't the creaky floor or the sound of a rat scampering across the room. It was laughter.

~*~

Days turned into weeks. I contacted my stepdad. We'd gone together to pick up Mom's/ not my mom's ashes. I kept her last words to myself, though, until I figured out how I was going to deal with it all. He took the urn. Thank God. No matter whatever happens between me and him, I'll always remember that. I just couldn't. I couldn't have her back in the house. I was still learning about hauntings and connecting with the other side. I didn't know if she could still get to me. I mean, she *could*, but I really hoped she couldn't.

I was meeting with a counselor three times a week. They got my meds straight and I was following the recommended dosage. I was trying. The pills, I hated them. I still thought they might poison me, leaving me in a sleeping death state, zoning out 24/7. I'd stopped buying wine. It wasn't helping with my mental state or with the uninvited house guests either. Per my therapist's instructions, I started exercising, deadlifting. My body was strong. My brain was super clear. I was feeling better every day, like I had superpowers like I knew the answers to everything.

Back to work at *BB's*, hi ho. The work was good, distracting. Bennie had leased the space next door where *Blue* had been. I wasn't quite sure what she was going to do with it, but I knew some kind of construction was going to start before school got out for the summer. Tristan had taken me under her wing like I was another kid. Who would have thought? She was a mom; she couldn't help herself. She told me everything about her new tattoo and all about The Order of Lilith. What with the Girls gone and Kelly...Kelly. I was still processing what happened to Kelly...I needed something to believe in. Lilith, a protector, a warrior, a witch. Where do I sign up?

I was closing up early at *BB's*. Close to finals, I needed to hit the books. Then the door opened. Could have sworn I'd locked it. Lavender in the air. Ro.

"The fuck, Ro. What are you doing here? I gotta jam. Finals and all, and oh yeah, I don't want to talk to you! Seriously, the fuck?"

She looked at me with those amber orbs, baby bangs framing her forehead, and her once black hair, now bleached and cropped into a bob. "Elia, please. Please let me explain."

I said nothing, but I didn't kick her out either.

"Elia, we needed you. Er, *they* needed you, The Five. Sure, I was a part of The Six then, but not anymore, though. At the time, I pretty much did whatever Luna told me to do. And your energy — we knew we could make something happen. YOU were the key to making it all work."

"And, what exactly did *I* help make work? I mean, what the hell happened that night?"

"That's just it, Elia. Nothing. Nothing that

I know of anyway. Sometimes, I think it's all just hocus pocus, glitter, and incense, costumes, pretend. The Five aren't hanging around anymore. I'm not welcome. They made that clear. And I talked to T..."

"You what? Again, the fuck, Ro?"

"I...I felt really bad about everything that went down between us. I didn't want you to think I was using you, but that's how it came across anyway. After T and I talked, I felt better."

I was fuming at this point.

"When I talked to T, she told me to be patient. And I have been. I want to be your friend, Elia."

"How the hell can I trust you?"

"I know. I know. It was shitty of me leading you on, but give me a chance. I want to be friends, k?"

Fuming less but still silent, I began to go about my closing duties, mentally checking things off in my head. I just let her stew. I'd done everything but turn out the lights and lock the door. She was still waiting around. Okay. Let me think. Did Ro ever cross any lines past harmless flirting? Lots of girls who were friends did that.

But, no, no, that wasn't her intention. She'd meant to lure me. I fell into the trap. I took the bait. I was past the attraction now, but...friends? And going to T. THAT was crossing a line.

Walking to the door, Ro followed. I opened it, stepping aside and letting her pass to the sidewalk. Still, she waited. I locked the door and turned towards her. I'd give her this. She was persistent.

"Look, Ro. I'm not making any promises. A lot has happened this year, and I'm still unpacking everything."

She nodded. "I'll take it. If that's where you are right now, I'll take it. I don't expect everything with The Five, uh, Six at the time, to magically disappear like it never happened. And my part in it. I am sorry, Elia."

"Well, it's not just what happened with The Six. I have a lot of other shit going on. But...I've fucked up a lot, and I mean a lot, and T has always just forgiven me, no questions asked. I'll have to ask her how she does it," I said, almost smiling. Almost.

"Good," was all she said, and I was left

standing there with only the faint hint of lavender left behind. No more cloves.

Walking home, I was thinking back. All of it, this last year of high school, the hurricane, my imagined relationship with Ro. I'd survived being hazed by The Satanic Six. Losing Kelly. That one still stung. And now, being motherless. It's amazing I'm doing as well as I am and not completely falling apart. My feet knew the way, taking me home. Home. Not a home with my real parents, but my home, nonetheless.

So many questions. I needed answers. The only place I could imagine finding anything relevant was in the attic, maybe in the BOOKS box. I hadn't been in the attic since Iris and Joyce had performed their ritual up there, clearing the space. We'd locked it up again, even. With the keys and a flashlight from the junk drawer in the kitchen, I headed upstairs.

The space was clean and unchanged. Nothing in there but the old trunk, the BOOKS, and that old vanity. Nothing else was in there. It was calm. And I hadn't felt any lasting calm in my house, well, ever. I sat down in front of the BOOK box and opened the top. It was easy. No tape. The flaps just folded in on one another. I began to take out book after book, stacking them beside me on the floor. Nothing very interesting. I was beginning to think these were only my Mom's/not my mom's college textbooks.

Then, at the bottom of the box, I found two scrapbooks. I put them to the side and repacked the others, taking my time. I was too afraid to open them and take a look. I didn't know what I would find. I didn't know if I was ready for the answers, the truth if it was in there. I just sat there with the scrapbooks in my lap, gripping the worn edges. Was I ready? And just before I opened the first one, I felt a gust of air move through me. It took my breath away. My hands flew to my heart. I wasn't scared, though. I felt peace. So strange. And I smelled...vanilla.

Aunt Laera.

CHAPTER 15

It was over. Senior year. So much had happened. T and I celebrated her 18th birthday last month — April 1st. My red-headed bestie, fire sign sister, was born on April Fool's Day. T's parents had a special dinner complete with champagne. But I passed on the alcohol. I wore the peachy sundress they'd given me last year for my birthday, well, with a black cardigan and my Docs. It was T's turn to get a car. It was waiting for her in the drive the morning of her big day. A big red bow atop the hood, just like on TV. T had *that* kind of family.

Exams were over. I'd finally turned in my senior piece. Self-portrait. A black and white skull, pills of many colors representing what would have been teeth. The mouth turned up in the corners, a maniacal smile. Dark, edgy, but art teachers liked that kind of thing. Prom was now in the past. We'd gone together, just T and me. I'd worn a new-to-me long black dress with a boho-looking fringed shawl, one large red rose embroidered in the center, *Rhiannon* on my mind. Kelly would have approved. T looked stunning in a long, pink vintage gown, something like Carrie's from, well, *Carrie*, minus the pig blood.

My stepdad came to graduation. He was the only family who came to see me walk across the stage. Not really my family. I hadn't brought that up with him yet. I did happen to spy Tristan and Bennie in the back of the auditorium. It was so crowded I couldn't get through the mass of people, and they left before I had a chance to see them. I'd catch them later at work. Speaking of work, Bennie had knocked down a wall expanding into the old *Blue* space, making room for more seating. She even had a reading nook in the corner, a lending library, shelves filled with board games, leftover beach reads, and some of the shop's old woo woo books. And next to the table closest to the shelves, there was a small sign that read Kelly's Corner. She was still there. Kelly. In spirit.

It felt like I had it all. The future was about to reveal itself, but for now, summer stretched out before us. There would be late movie nights and pizza from Frank's. We'd walk by the water, the air stagnant, sweltering, ice cream dripping down our hands, hitting the hot sidewalk faster than we could eat it, making creamy puddles, swirls of chocolate and vanilla. Some days, we'd just sit and watch the sunset, holding hands like Thelma and Louise. We'd stay 'til the sun disappeared at the horizon's edge, dusk setting in with the purples and pinks of twilight. T and I knew that she'd be off to university, leaving me with the locals in our quaint, bayside town. I'd start at the community college and keep working at *BB's*. I'd even talked to Bennie about working at the sister location, *Beach Bum's,* on the island. Now that school was out and I had my own wheels, I could use a change of scenery.

With Tristan's help, I learned more about The Order of Lilith. She and Bennie were the only woo woo connection I had left in town, but maybe Iris and Joyce, too? And Ro? Shit. I still wasn't sure about her. Anyway, I hoped that maybe soon we'd start some kind of gatherings or circles. I needed that.

T was going with me to my appointment. I was getting new ink. My first tattoo! Now, I would be linked to Bennie, Tristan, Kelly, my Aunt Laera, all of the witchy women who felt Lilith's pull. I liked the idea of balance, fairness, and justice—I needed that too. Rae worked at *Salt Life Ink*. She came into *BB's* for coffee, a regular. She'd be the artist working on me. I decided to get the incircle on the back of my right calf above my ankle, a place that wouldn't show with my Docs and a place I was still comfortable exposing without them.

The *Salt Life* was downtown, a couple of blocks from *BB's*. I was wearing my Aunt Laera's dark vintage dress with the drop waist and the pearl buttons I'd found in the attic. T was just trying to survive the summer in cut-offs and a tank top. She'd chosen function over fashion today. The shop was bright, the walls crowded with custom work and band posters, Margo Price's cover of *Two Headed Dog* blaring over the vibratory sounds of machines, permanently marking locals and tourists alike. It hurt. I'm not gonna lie, but I handled it. It was worth it. It didn't take long and after Rae applied the clear bandage, she went over care instructions with me. I was no stranger to wound care, but this was a little different.

We walked out, heading down the sidewalk

to go pick up a couple of cold coffees for the trek home.

"Wow!" T said, "That is really cool, Elia. But I don't think I could stomach the pain." T wrapped both arms around her middle, bent over, and pretended to puke.

"Yeah. I don't know. You may be stronger than you think. You're my closest friend, after all and I'm kind of a lot of work. If you can handle me, I think you could grin and bear getting a tattoo!" I gave her a wink.

Heading for *BB's*, we were laughing and giving each other friendly shoves from side to side. I noticed a guy leaning up against the wall, not far from *Salt Life*, thumbs in his belt loops, smoking a cigarette. No hint of cloves in the air here. Straight up, Marlboro, man. Was he giving me the up/down? He was surrounded by a pack of guys, all looking like they stepped right out of a 1950s biker flick. Usually, I'd look away, but my eyes met his, and I didn't drop the gaze even as T and I passed them. I kept glancing over my shoulder until I couldn't turn my head any farther.

"T. T. Did you see that guy?"

T just shrugged and kept going on about what flavor she might get in her frappe.

I stopped her then. "T, no, wait, did you see them, those guys we walked by a minute ago?"

"Uh, no. I wasn't looking, and anyway, Elia, you know better than to go around with any guys like that."

"Ha!" I said. "So, you *did* see them!"

"Well, yes, but I didn't spend any time looking at them or thinking about them. What gives anyway?"

T was focused on getting out of town and off to college. She was not going to waste her time this summer having a fling or getting involved with anybody. But me, on the other hand...I had nothing to lose. I hadn't been interested in anybody since the Ro bullshit. I tried to be sly, look back, and check him out. Ugh. Busted. He was still staring at me. He took one more drag from his cigarette, squashed it under his boot, smiled, and turned back to his friends, just leaving me with the view of the back of his head, his dark, chestnut hair pulled into a short, low ponytail at the nape of his neck. Shit. Whoa. I felt flushed. Even in this heat, I felt hot. And…interested.

T yanked me by the arm at that point, pulling me out of my brief stupor. "C'mon. Let's get to *BB*'s and into the freakin' AC. I'm dying out here! And let me add something, Elia. You're my friend, and I think I can be straight with you. If, and I mean if, you even think about going after one of those guys, be careful. Use your head. And another thing, shower. You reek, girl."

T and I parted at the crossroads. I walked just a little way more and then I was home. Home. My home. Since getting back to regular with my counseling sessions, following the dosage with my meds, and ditching the habit of losing myself nightly in glasses, er bottles, of red wine, my house *did* feel more like home. Putting the experience with The Six, well, I made Seven behind me, I was slowly getting my act together. I was even keeping the house clean, sweeping, dusting, and washing my clothes more regularly. I didn't know what T was talking about, my needing a shower. I stuck my nose down my dress. I didn't smell anything unusual.

On my way to bed, I stopped in the

bathroom. No sign of Aunt Laera or any gross shit coming out of the faucets lately. I hoped she wasn't gone for good, though. I still wanted to go through those old scrapbooks, look for clues and information, and try to figure out where I came from, but not tonight. I washed up and looked in the mirror as I toweled off my hands and face. My dark hair framing my face and eyes. I touched my jawline, turning my head left and right, noticing. Even though I was good about SPF coverage, my vampire-like skin had a rosy glow in the apples of my cheeks. And another thing, my eyes, the eyes we all shared, all of The Horrifying Women, were clear, cornflower blue shining back at me, the fogginess gone. Out of my haze. For once, I liked what I saw. Maybe that's what *he* had seen, too.

Stretching out in my bed, surrounded by my purple walls, I went over the events of the afternoon, thinking about *him*. Maybe I'd run into *him* again. I needed to go back to see Rae after my new ink healed so she could inspect her work. Maybe he'd be there, hanging out again like the ghost of James Dean. I needed to at least find out his name. Then, I heard "Letty" like a whisper in the air. Was that it? Was his name Letty? How weird. Must be some sixth sense kicking in from years of dabbling in the woo. Letty, huh.

Smiling to myself, I was just about to drop off when I heard something else. It sounded like footsteps on the stairs. The hair on my neck was tickling me, and my arms broke out in goosies. The fuck? I tiptoed out of my room and into the hall, peering around the corner. I made my way slowly down the stairs, flipping on light switches and walking through rooms. Hmm. Nothing. I decided to get some water to take back to my room. I took a sip and then set the glass down on the counter. That's when I saw it. Crumbs. I know I'd wiped the kitchen down this morning, and I hadn't eaten anything else here. Picking up a few morsels, bits sticking to my fingers, I was about to inspect the tiny grains when a blast of cold air shot past me, leaving behind a distinct odor and not a pleasant one. Bringing my fingertips to my tongue, I tasted the remains.

Shit.

Fucking cheesecake.

ACKNOWLEDGEMENTS

Hazed is the second novella following *Wounded*. Whereas *Wounded* originated from a place of personal pain, *Hazed* took on a life of its own. The characters were born in Elia's world, and as the voices talked, I listened. They have their own stories to share, and I hope I did them justice.

I'd like to thank Lylith Nyx for her friendship and for being an early reader of my work and giving me great insight and loving support. Much appreciation goes out to Delliom Ellidom for spending the time to not only read my manuscript but also for offering thoughtful suggestions. Truly, your extra eyes were appreciated. Adam Martin, you've done it again! Thank you for creating my cover art. You take my simple ideas and turn them into something beautiful and haunting. Looking forward to future collaborations! I extend much gratitude to Paulette Kennedy for reading and blurbing my book. After reading your book, *The Devil and Mrs. Davenport*, I can say I am truly honored that you offered your time and talents to little old me. And a special thank you to Karen Fuller, my editor, and to World Castle Publishing for taking a chance on a new author and making my work a polished product.

Hazed is dedicated to my daughters, Amelia and Meredith. You are two of my best teachers. Thanks for making me a mother. I am inspired every day to get better at it.

Lastly, I thank my husband, Don. We are partners in this life, happening to it on a regular basis. Here's to the future and many more adventures. Of course, quiet evenings with popcorn and a spooky show are the best!

About the Author

Greta T. Bates resides in a quaint, coastal town and considers herself a beach person. A winter beach person. Summer finds her indoors, writing and editing and waiting for fall. She writes stories that explore lost love, revenge, and the struggle of being a human, told through the lens of horror. A Mills College alumna, she has been featured in several online publications, and her poetry can be found in *Dream*, 2nd edition, and *Shards*, both publications of Ravens Quoth Press.

Greta's short stories can be found in *Horror Scope-A Zodiac Anthology*, volumes 1 and 3, *Pretty Girls Make Graves*, and *Till the Yule Log Burns Out*. Her latest short story, *Look-alike*, can be found in *Dolls in the Attic*. She is the proud author of *Wounded*.

Currently, she is working on her second novel. Greta lives on the Gulf Coast with her small fam, 3 cats, and her little dog, too.

Hazed is her second novella.

Website and social link:
https://gretabateswrites.wixsite.com/gretatbatesauthor
www.instagram.com/greta_t_bates

www.ingramcontent.com/pod-product-compliance
Lightning Source LLC
Chambersburg PA
CBHW030224180626
46810CB00008B/2949